nickelodeon™ PANDEMONIUM!

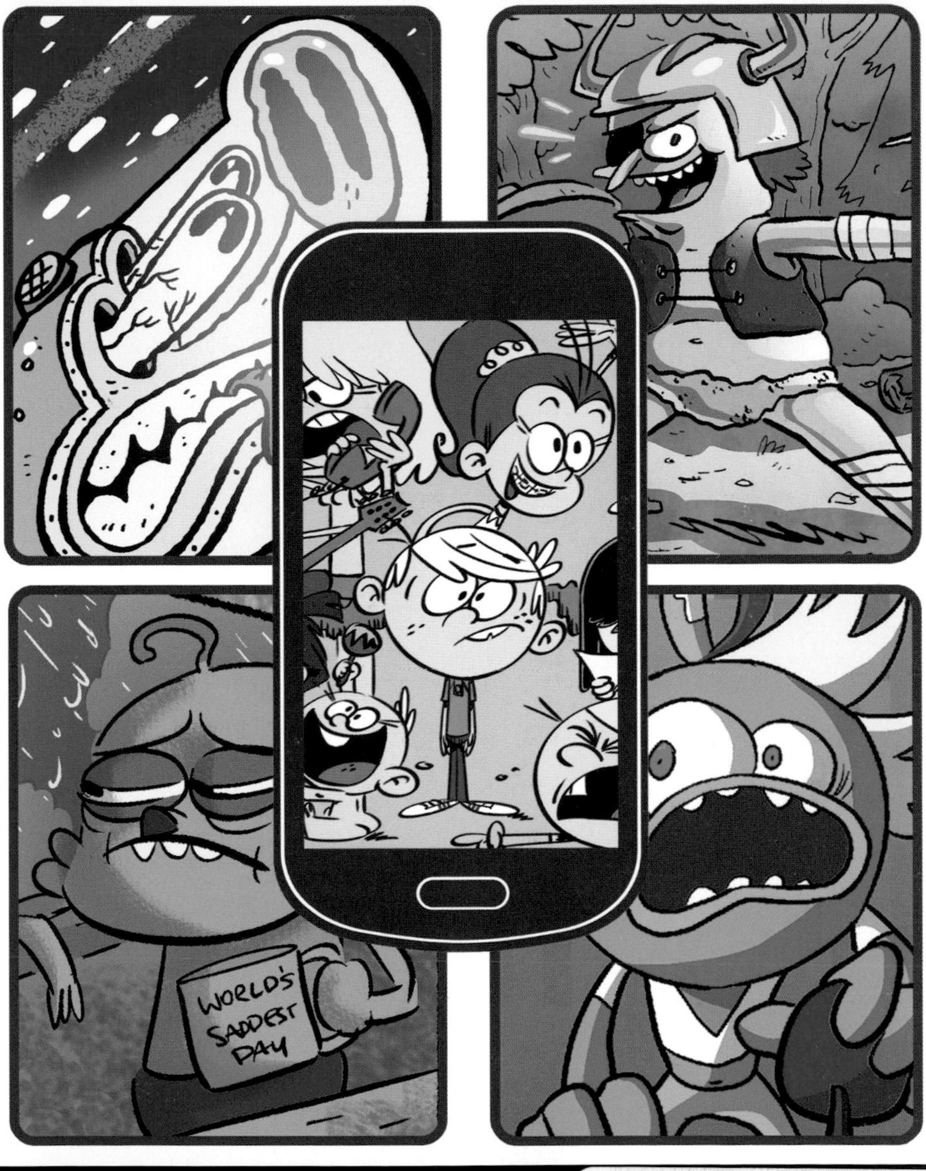
WORLD'S SADDEST DAY

PAPERCUT
New York

nickelodeon GRAPHIC NOVELS AVAILABLE FROM PAPERCUTZ

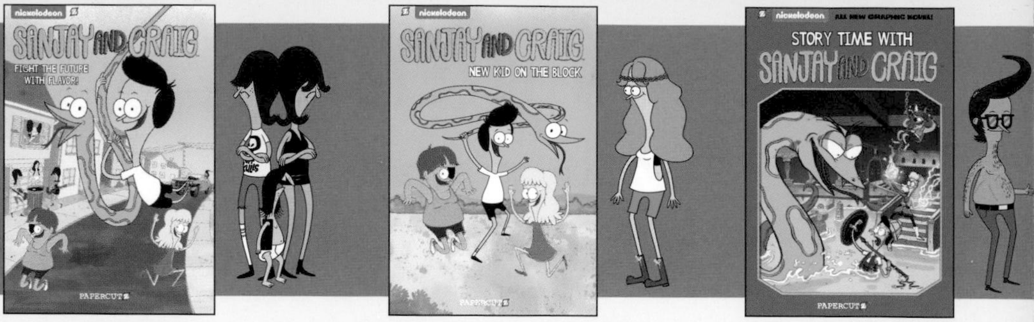
SANJAY AND CRAIG
FIGHT THE FUTURE WITH FLAVOR!
PAPERCUTZ
SANJAY AND CRAIG
NEW KID ON THE BLOCK
PAPERCUTZ
STORY TIME WITH
SANJAY AND CRAIG
PAPERCUTZ

SANJAY AND CRAIG
#1 "Fight the Future with Flavor"

SANJAY AND CRAIG
#2 "New Kid on the Block"

SANJAY AND CRAIG
#3 "Story Time with Sanjay and Craig"

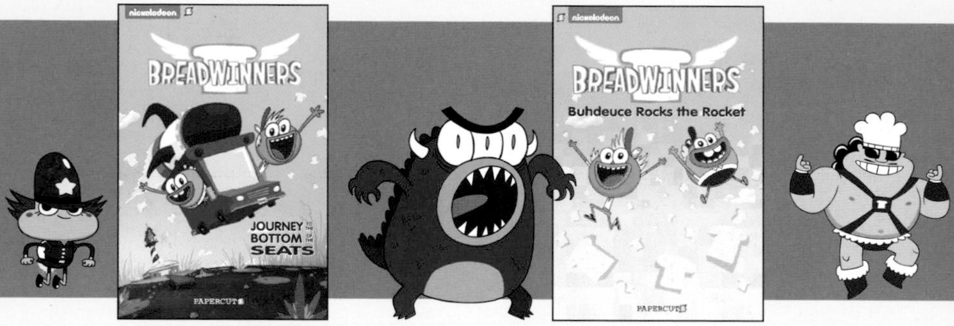
BREADWINNERS
JOURNEY TO THE BOTTOM OF THE SEATS
PAPERCUTZ
BREADWINNERS
Buhdeuce Rocks the Rocket
PAPERCUTZ

BREADWINNERS
#1 "Journey to the Bottom of the Seats"

BREADWINNERS
#2 "Buhdeuce Rocks the Rocket"

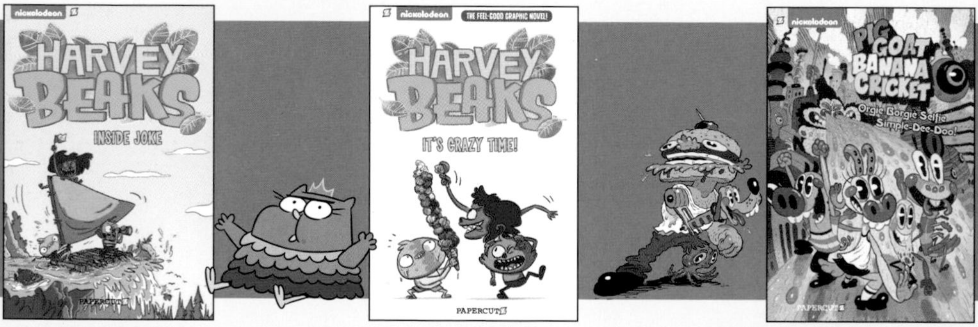
HARVEY BEAKS
INSIDE JOKE
PAPERCUTZ
THE FEEL-GOOD GRAPHIC NOVEL!
HARVEY BEAKS
IT'S CRAZY TIME!
PAPERCUTZ
PIG GOAT BANANA CRICKET
Orgle Borgle Selfie Simple-Dee-Doo!
PAPERCUTZ

HARVEY BEAKS
#1 "Inside Joke"

HARVEY BEAKS
#2 "It's Crazy Time"

PIG GOAT BANANA CRICKET
#1 "Orgle Borgle Selfie Simple-Dee Doo!"

Nickelodeon graphic novels are available for $7.99 in paperback, $12.99 in hardcover. Available from booksellers everywhere. You can also order online from papercutz.com, or call 1-800-886-1223, Monday through Friday, 9-5 EST. MC, Visa, and AmEx accepted. To order by mail, please add $4.00 for postage and handling for first book ordered, $1.00 for each additional book and make check payable to NBM Publishing.
Send to: Papercutz, 160 Broadway, Suite 700, East Wing, New York, NY 10038.

Nickelodeon graphic novels are also available digitally wherever e-books are sold.

nickelodeon™
PANDEMONIUM!

CHANNELING FUN

TUFF	**5**	**SANJAY AND CRAIG** New Hector gets carried away LARPing.
BIO	**13**	**TOON TALK** New An animated discussion with Dave Cooper, the co-creator of PIG GOAT BANANA CRICKET.
FUN	**15**	**SUMMER FUN** Rerun Suggestions from Pig, Goat, Banana, and Cricket.
LOAF	**16**	**BREADWINNERS** Rerun SwaySway and Buhdeuce pack bread.
TREE	**17**	**HARVEY BEAKS** New Harvey, Fee, and Foo create a TV network.
BIO	**25**	**TOON TALK** New C. H. Greenblatt spills the beans on creating Harvey Beaks.
SCI	**27**	**SCIENCE CORNER** New Cricket explains stuff to you.
LOAF	**28**	**BREADWINNERS** New "Tadpolice." Whatcha gonna do when they come for you?
BIO	**37**	**TOON TALK** New Share a slice of life with Breadwinners co-creator Steve Borst.
FUN	**39**	**SUMMER FUN** Rerun Harvey Beak's summer fun suggestion: "Go jump in a lake!"
PGBC	**40**	**PIG GOAT BANANA CRICKET** New Guest-starring Quandarious Gooch. The roommates join their Cable TV hero's live reality show.
BIO	**53**	**TOON TALK** New PGBC co-creator Johnny Ryan reveals who he met at Angouleme, France!
TREE	**55**	**FOO FACTS** Rerun Foo explains computers to you.
FAM	**56**	**MEET THE LOUD FAMILY** Rerun Lincoln Loud has a lot of sisters.
FAM	**57**	**LOUD HOUSE** Rerun "Lincoln Loud's ABCs of Getting the Last Slice." The title says it all.
BIO	**62**	**TOON TALK** New Chris Savino, creator of The Loud House, reveals the inspiration for his show.
Z	**64**	**WATCH OUT FOR PAPERCUTZ** New Editor-in-Chief Jim Salicrup warns against the dangers of slicing fingers on comics.

nickelodeon

PANDEMONIUM!

#1 "CHANNELING FUN"

"WHEREFORE ART THOU, TUFFLIPS?"
Eric Esquivel - Writer
James Kaminski – Artist
Laurie E. Smith – Colorist
Tom Orzechowski – Letterer

"TADPOLICE"
Eric Esquivel – Writer
Allison Strejlau – Artist
Laurie E. Smith – Colorist
Tom Orzechowski – Letterer

" PUNCHLORD THE BLUDGEONER"
Eric Esquivel - Writer
Sam Spina - Artist & Letterer
Laurie E. Smith – Colorist

"MAKING A SPLASH"
Carson Montgomery – Writer
Andreas Schuster – Artist, Letterer
Matt Herms – Colorist

"SUMMER TREATS TO BEAT THE HEAT"
Eric Esquivel – Writer
Derek Fridolfs – Artist
Matteo Baldrighi – Colorist
Tom Orzechowski – Letterer

"QUANDARIOUS GOOCH"
Eric Esquivel – Writer
David DeGrand – Artist
Matt Herms – Colorist
Tom Orzechowski – Letterer

"HEAVY LOAF"
Stefan Petchua – Writer
Allison Strejlau – Artist
Laurie E. Smith – Colorist
Tom Orzechowski – Letterer

"CHANNELING FUN"
Kevin Kramer – Writer
Andreas Schuster – Artist and Letterer
Laurie E. Smith – Colorist

"FOO FACTS #89 – COMPUTERS"
Carson Montgomery – Writer
Andreas Schuster – Artist, letterer, colorist

"CRICKET'S SCIENCE CORNER: INSTRUMENTS"
Eric Esquivel – Writer
David DeGrand – Artist
Wes Dzioba – Colorist
Tom Orzechowski – Letterer

"ABCS OF GETTING THE LAST SLICE"
Chris Savino – Writer, artist
Jordan Rosato – Artist
Amanda Rynda – Colorist

Breadwinners created by Gary "Doodles" DiRaffeale and Steve Borst
Harvey Beaks created by C.H. Greenblatt
Pig Goat Banana Cricket created by Johnny Ryan and Dave Cooper
Sanjay and Craig created by Jim Dirschberger, Jay Howell, and Andreas Trolf
The Loud House created by Chris Savino

JAMES SALERNO – SR. ART DIRECTOR/NICKELODEON
CAITLIN HINRICHS – DESIGN/PRODUCTION
BRITTANIE BLACK – PRODUCTION COORDINATOR
EMELYNE TAN – EDITORIAL INTERN
BETHANY BRYAN
JEFF WHITMAN – EDITORS
JOAN HILTY – COMICS EDITOR/NICKELODEON
JIM SALICRUP
EDITOR-IN-CHIEF

ISBN: 978-1- 62991-612- 5 paperback edition
ISBN: 978-1- 62991-613- 2 hardcover edition

Papercutz books may be purchased for business or promotional use. For information on bulk purchases please contact Macmillan Corporate and Premium Sales Department at (800) 221-7945 x5442.

Printed in China
October 2016 by O.G. Printing Productions, LTD.

Distributed by Macmillan
First Printing

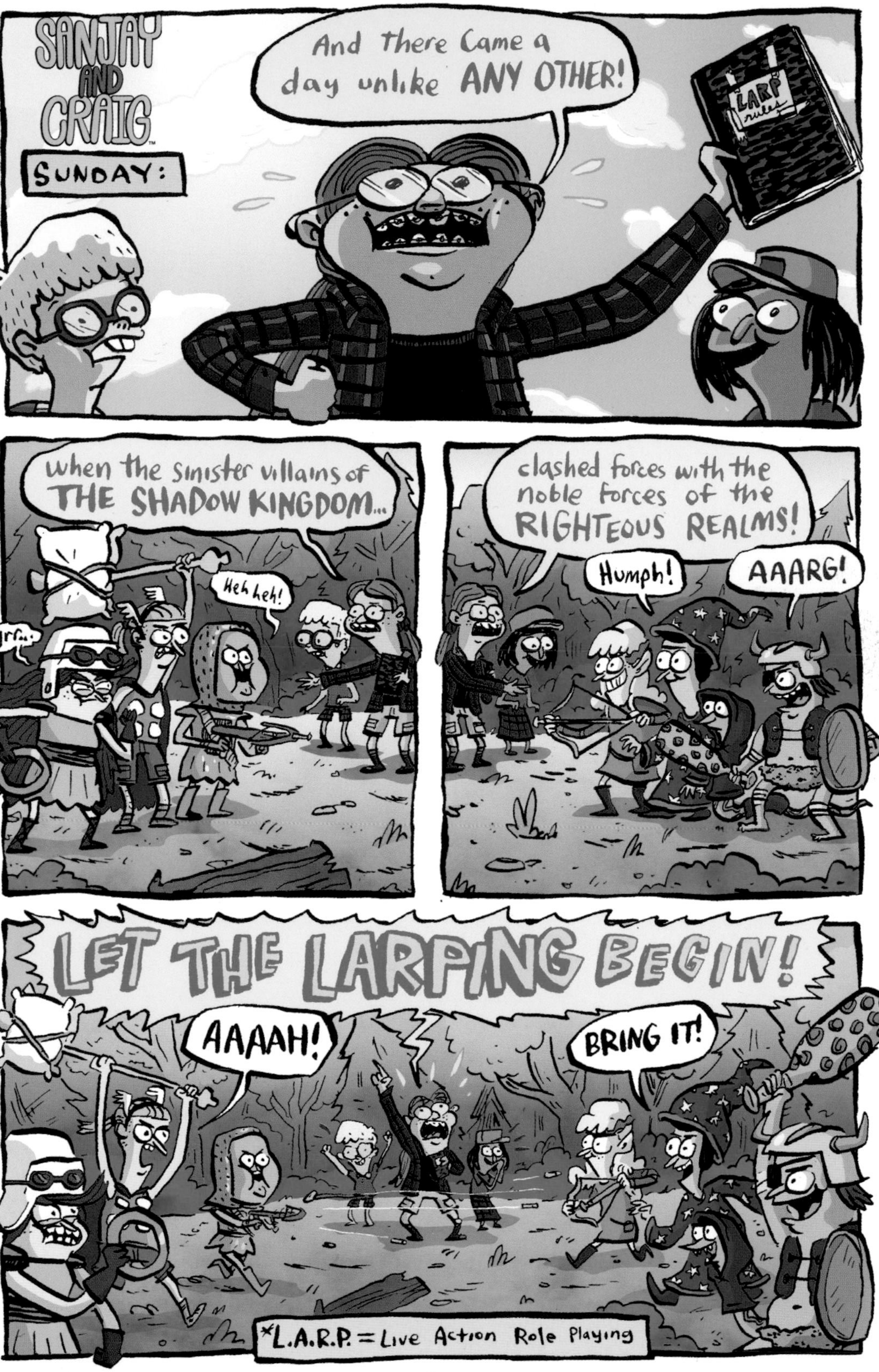
SANJAY AND CRAIG
SUNDAY:
And there came a day unlike ANY OTHER!
LARP rules
when the sinister villains of THE SHADOW KINGDOM...
grr...
Heh heh!
clashed forces with the noble forces of the RIGHTEOUS REALMS!
Humph!
AAARG!
LET THE LARPING BEGIN!
AAAAH!
BRING IT!
*L.A.R.P. = Live Action Role Playing

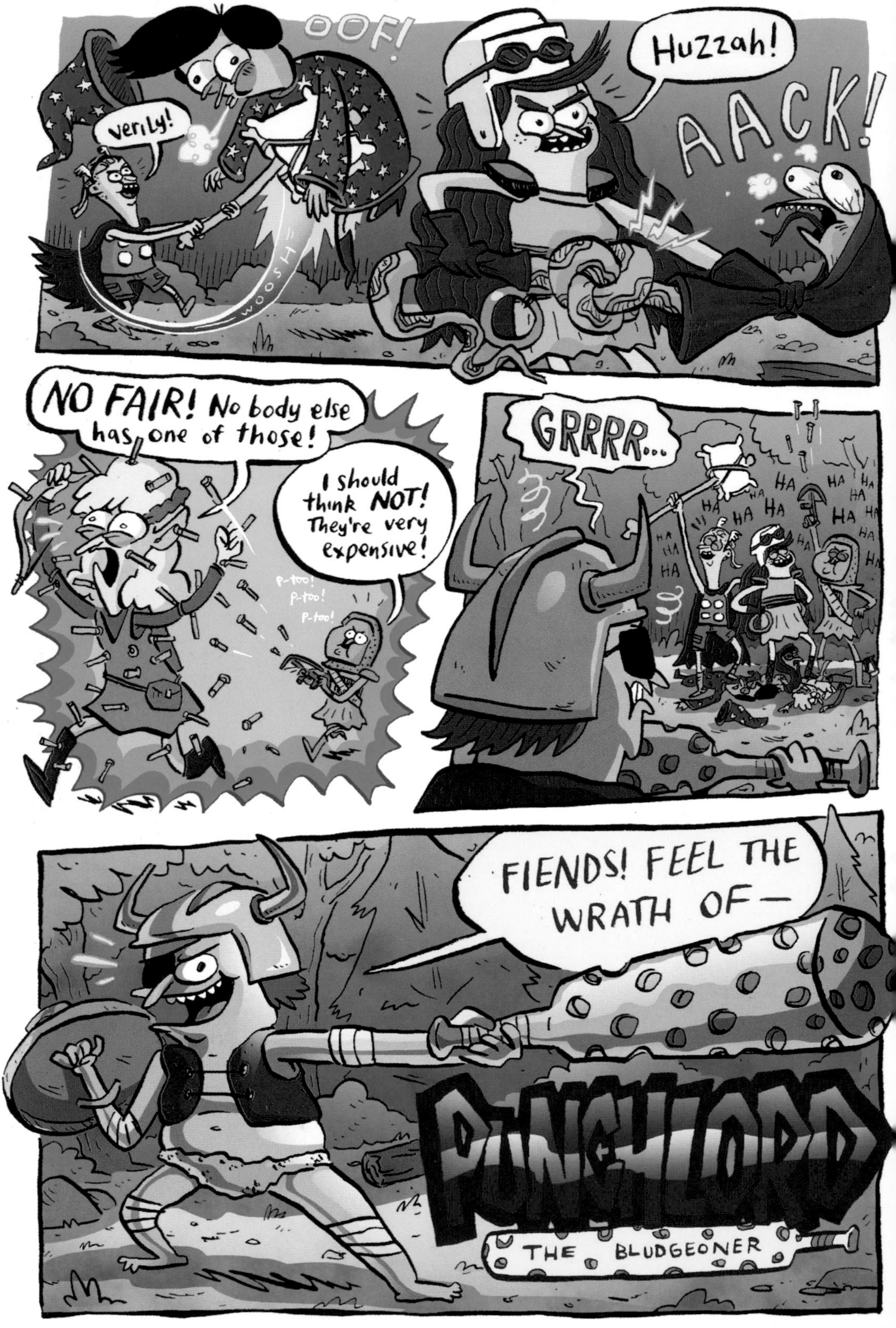
OOF!
verily!
WOOSH
Huzzah!
AACK!
NO FAIR! No body else has one of those!
I should think NOT! They're very expensive!
P-too!
P-too!
P-too!
GRRRR...
HA HA HA HA HA HA HA HA HA HA HA HA HA HA HA
FIENDS! FEEL THE WRATH OF—
PUNCHLORD
THE BLUDGEONER

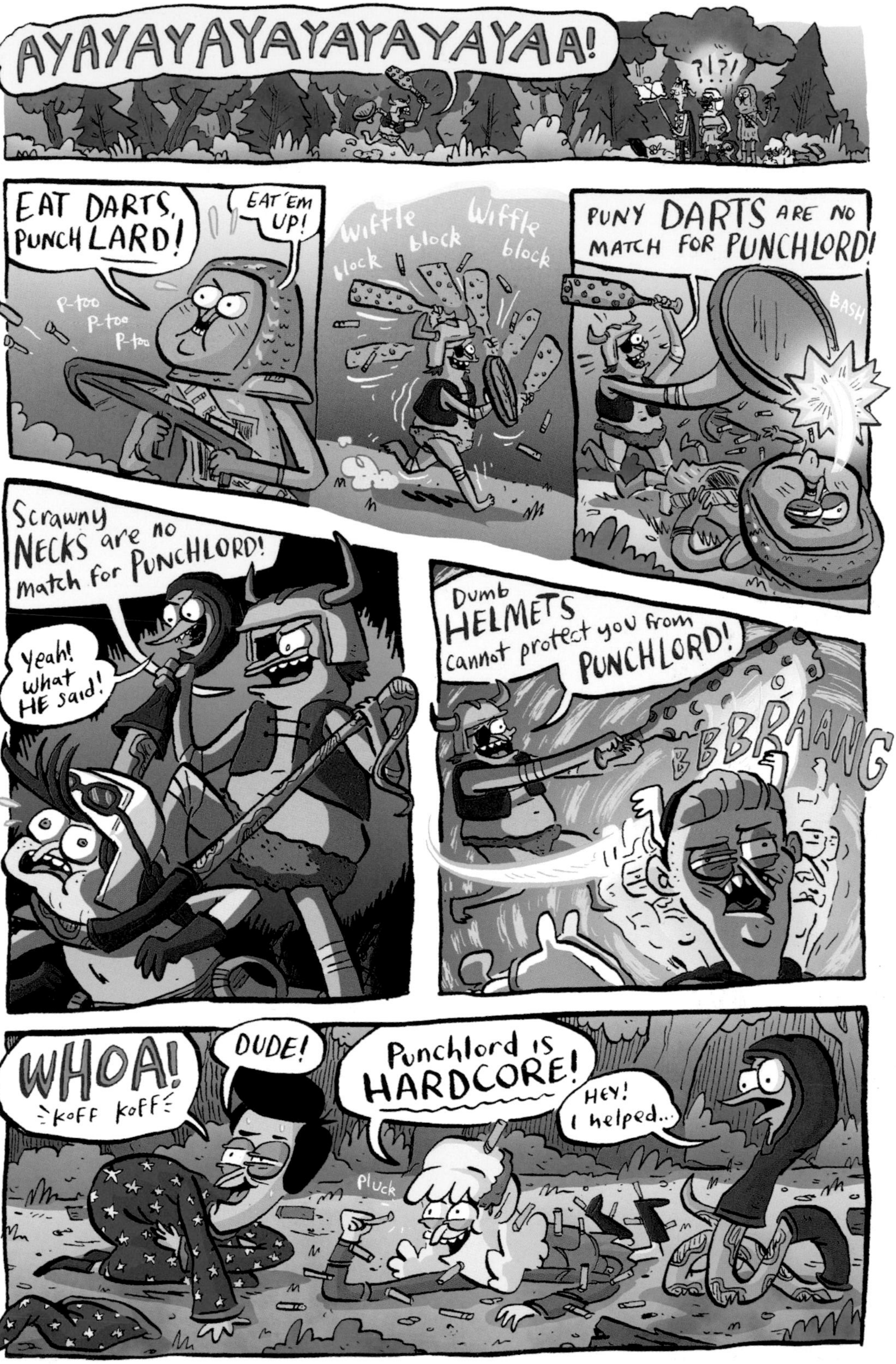

AYAYAYAYAYAYAYAYAYAA!
?!?!
EAT DARTS, PUNCH LARD!
EAT 'EM UP!
P-too P-too P-too
Wiffle block Wiffle block block
PUNY DARTS ARE NO MATCH FOR PUNCHLORD!
BASH
Scrawny NECKS are no match for PUNCHLORD!
Yeah! What HE said!
Dumb HELMETS cannot protect you from PUNCHLORD!
BBBRAANG
WHOA! koff koff
DUDE!
Punchlord is HARDCORE!
pluck
HEY! I helped...

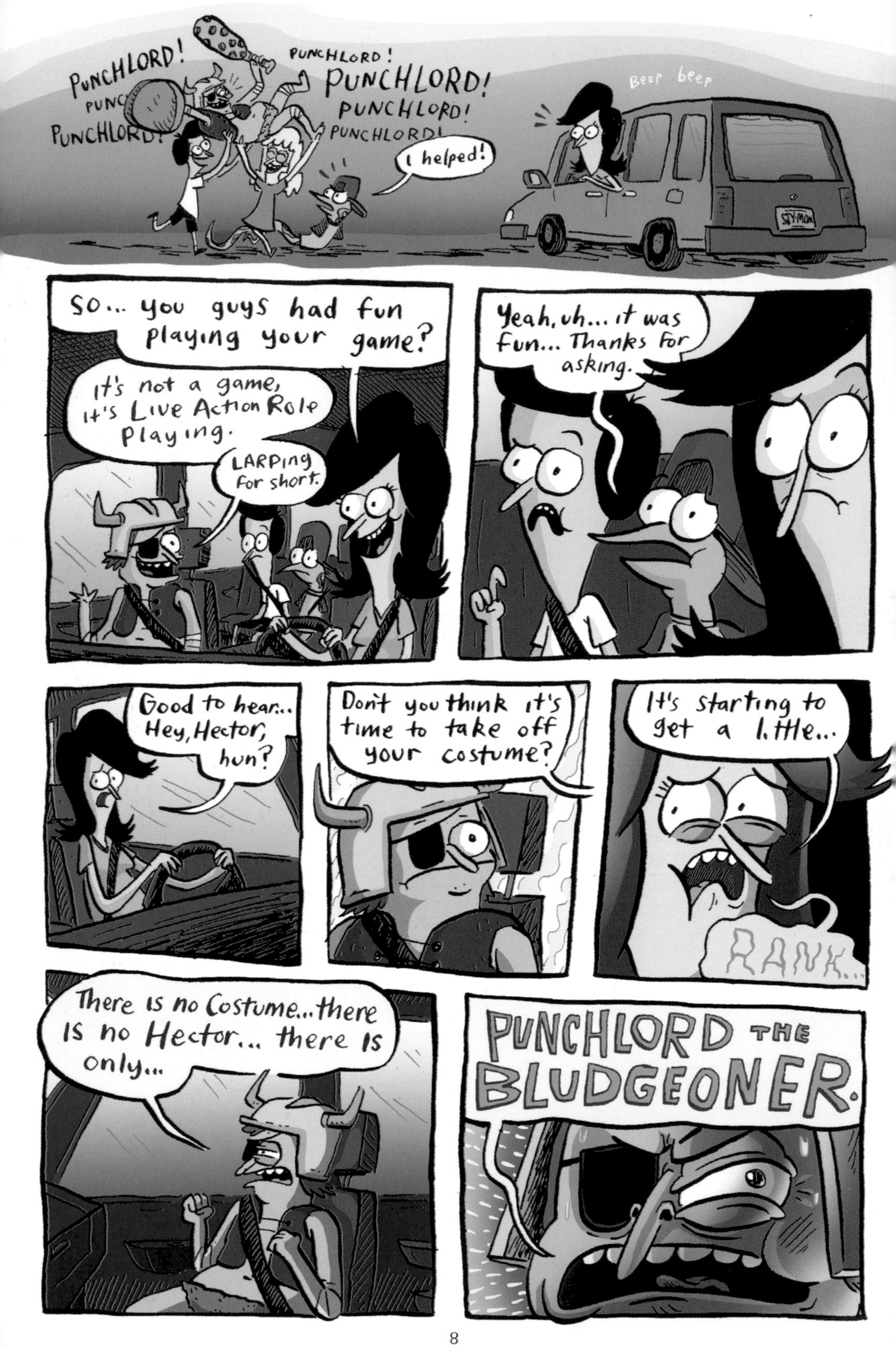
PUNCHLORD!
PUNC
PUNCHLORD!
PUNCHLORD!
PUNCHLORD!
PUNCHLORD!
PUNCHLORD!
I helped!
Beep beep
SO... you guys had fun playing your game?
It's not a game, it's Live Action Role Playing.
LARPing for short.
Yeah, uh... it was fun... Thanks for asking.
Good to hear... Hey, Hector, hun?
Don't you think it's time to take off your costume?
It's starting to get a little...
RANK...
There is no Costume... there is no Hector... there is only...
PUNCHLORD THE BLUDGEONER.

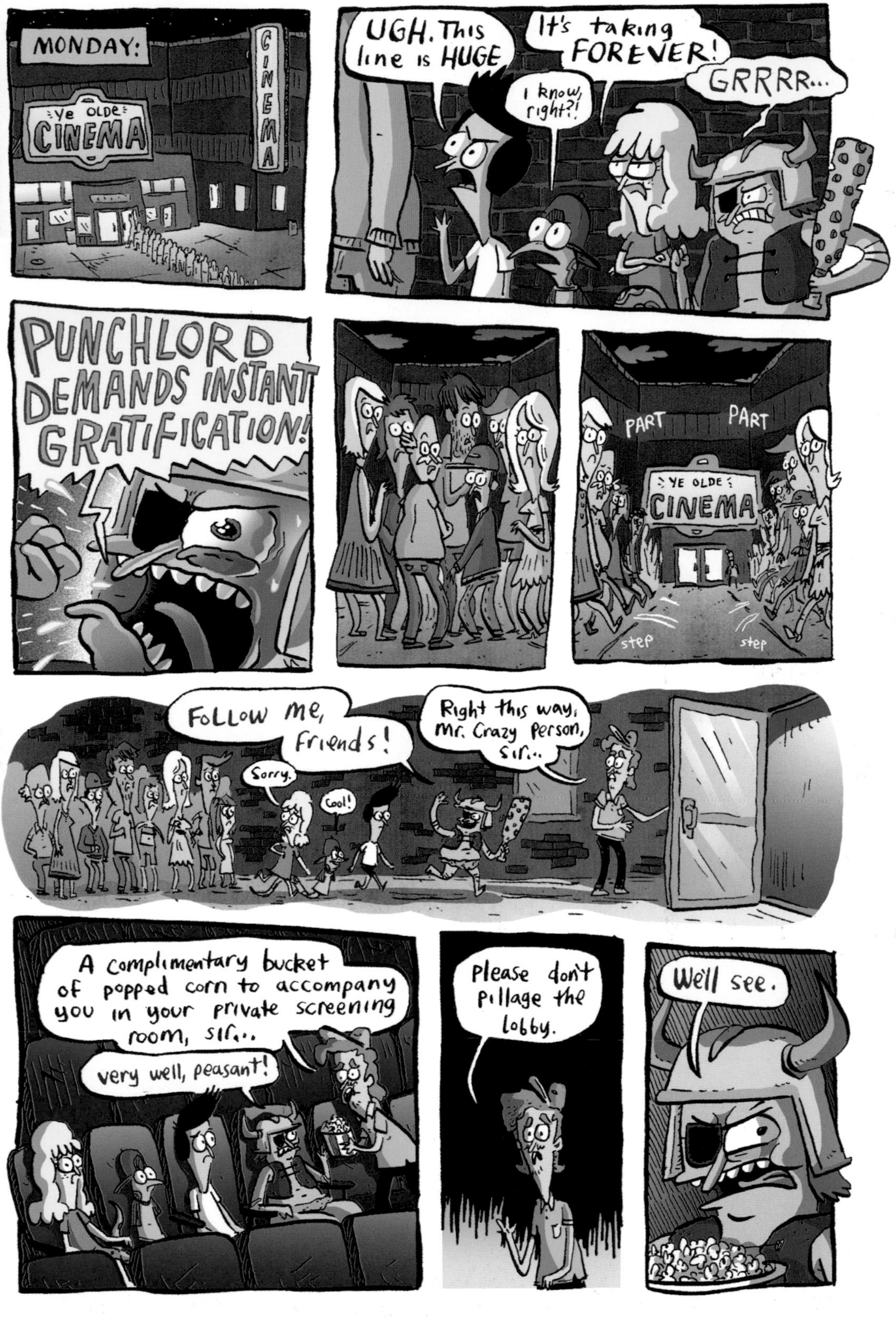
MONDAY:
YE OLDE CINEMA
CINEMA
UGH. This line is HUGE
It's taking FOREVER!
I know, right?!
GRRRR...
PUNCHLORD DEMANDS INSTANT GRATIFICATION!
PART
PART
YE OLDE CINEMA
step
step
Follow me, friends!
Right this way, Mr. Crazy Person, sir...
Sorry.
Cool!
A complimentary bucket of popped corn to accompany you in your private screening room, sir...
very well, peasant!
Please don't pillage the lobby.
We'll see.

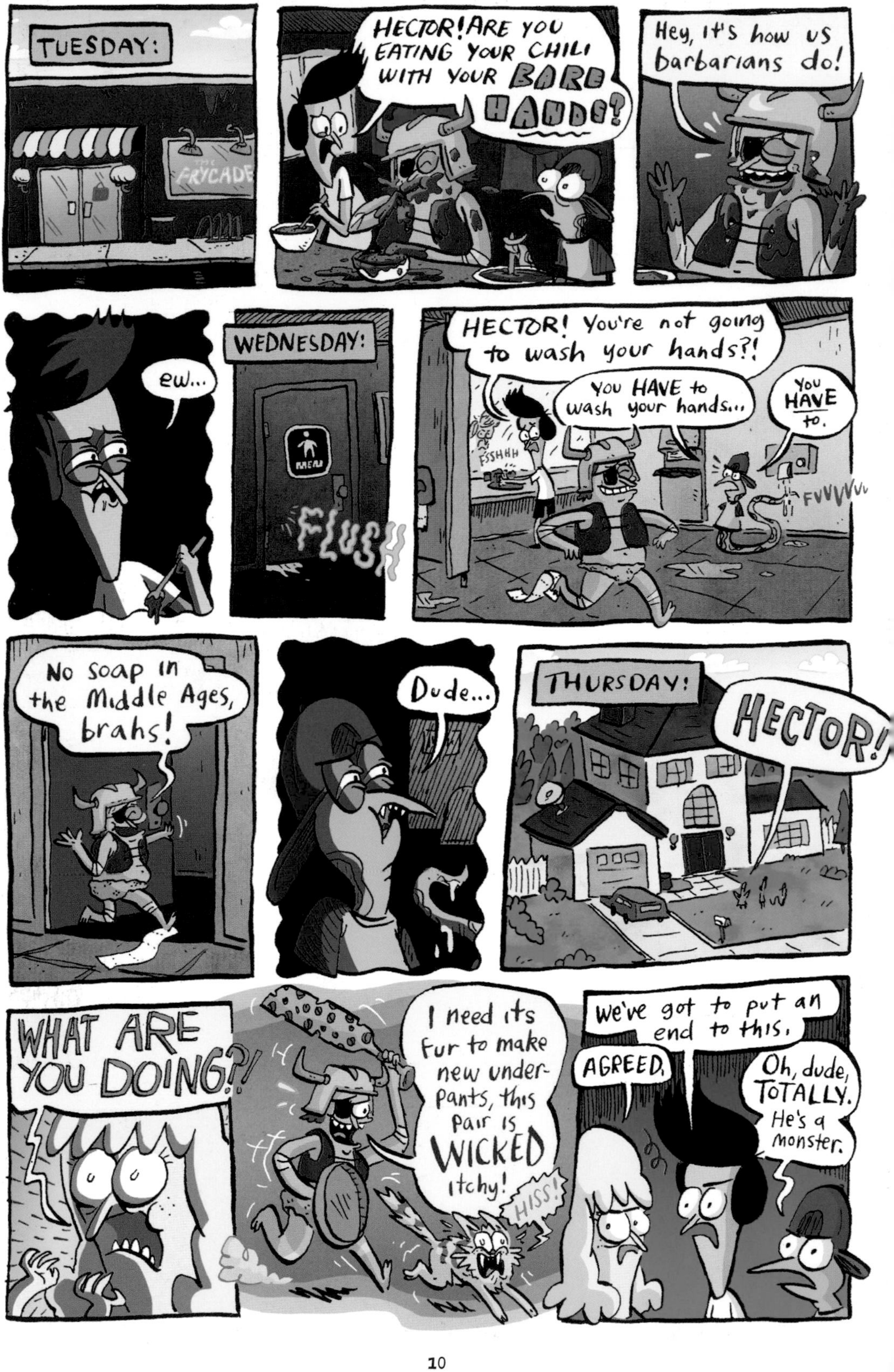
TUESDAY:
THE FRYCADE
HECTOR! ARE YOU EATING YOUR CHILI WITH YOUR BARE HANDS?
Hey, it's how us barbarians do!
ew...
WEDNESDAY:
MEN
FLUSH
HECTOR! You're not going to wash your hands?!
You HAVE to wash your hands...
You HAVE to.
FSSHHH
FVVVVVV
No soap in the Middle Ages, brahs!
Dude...
THURSDAY:
HECTOR!
WHAT ARE YOU DOING?!
I need its fur to make new underpants, this pair is WICKED itchy!
HISS!
We've got to put an end to this.
AGREED.
Oh, dude, TOTALLY. He's a monster.

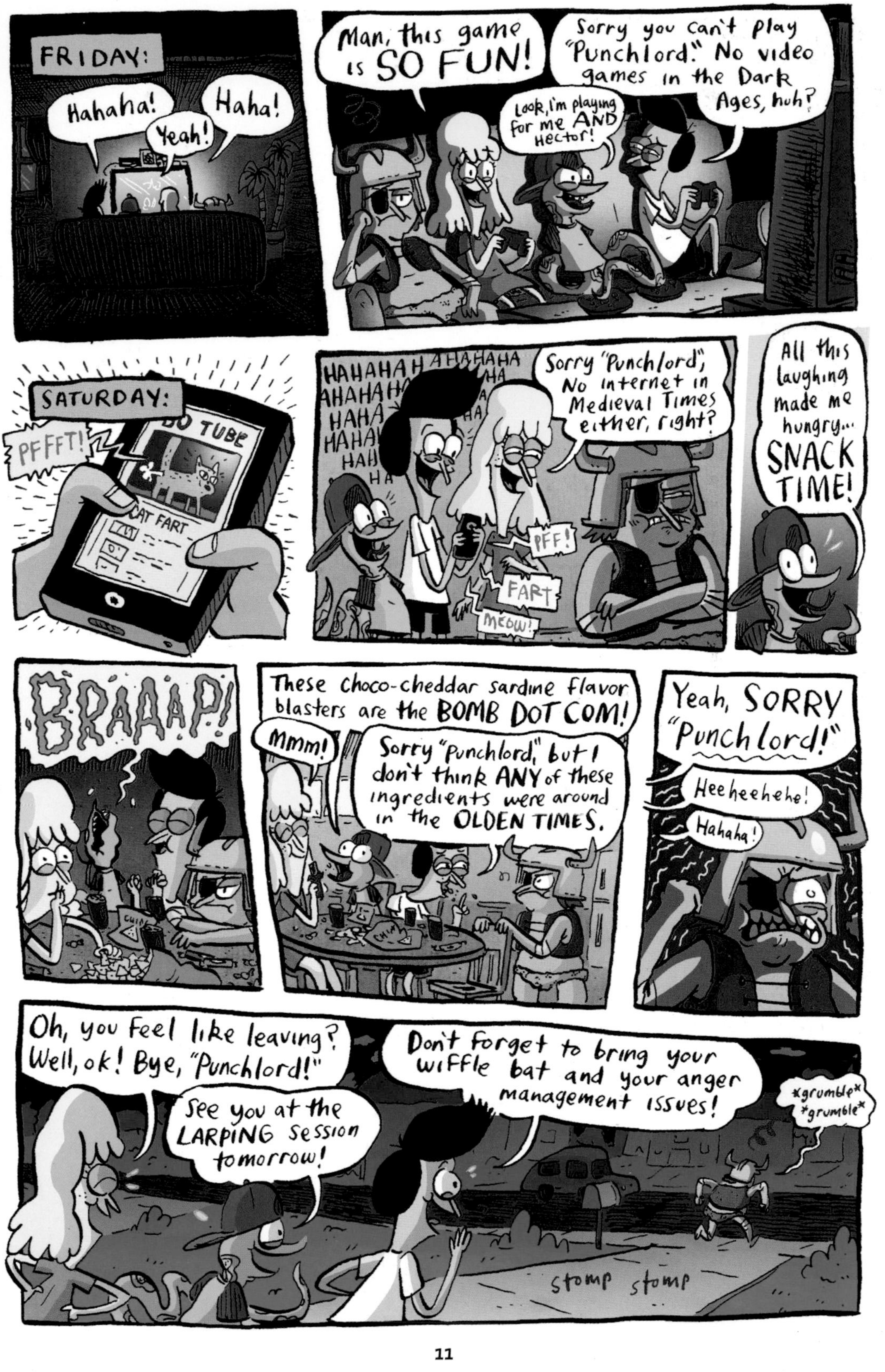
FRIDAY:
Hahaha!
Yeah!
Haha!
Man, this game is SO FUN!
Sorry you can't play "Punchlord." No video games in the Dark Ages, huh?
Look, I'm playing for me AND Hector!
SATURDAY:
PFFFT!
DO TUBE
CAT FART
HAHAHAHAHAHAHA
Sorry "Punchlord", No internet in Medieval Times either, right?
PFF!
FART
MEOW!
All this laughing made me hungry... SNACK TIME!
BRAAAP!
These choco-cheddar sardine flavor blasters are the BOMB DOT COM!
Mmm!
Sorry "punchlord," but I don't think ANY of these ingredients were around in the OLDEN TIMES.
Yeah, SORRY "Punchlord!"
Heeheehehe!
Hahaha!
Oh, you feel like leaving? Well, ok! Bye, "Punchlord!"
See you at the LARPING session tomorrow!
Don't forget to bring your wiffle bat and your anger management issues!
grumble *grumble*
stomp stomp

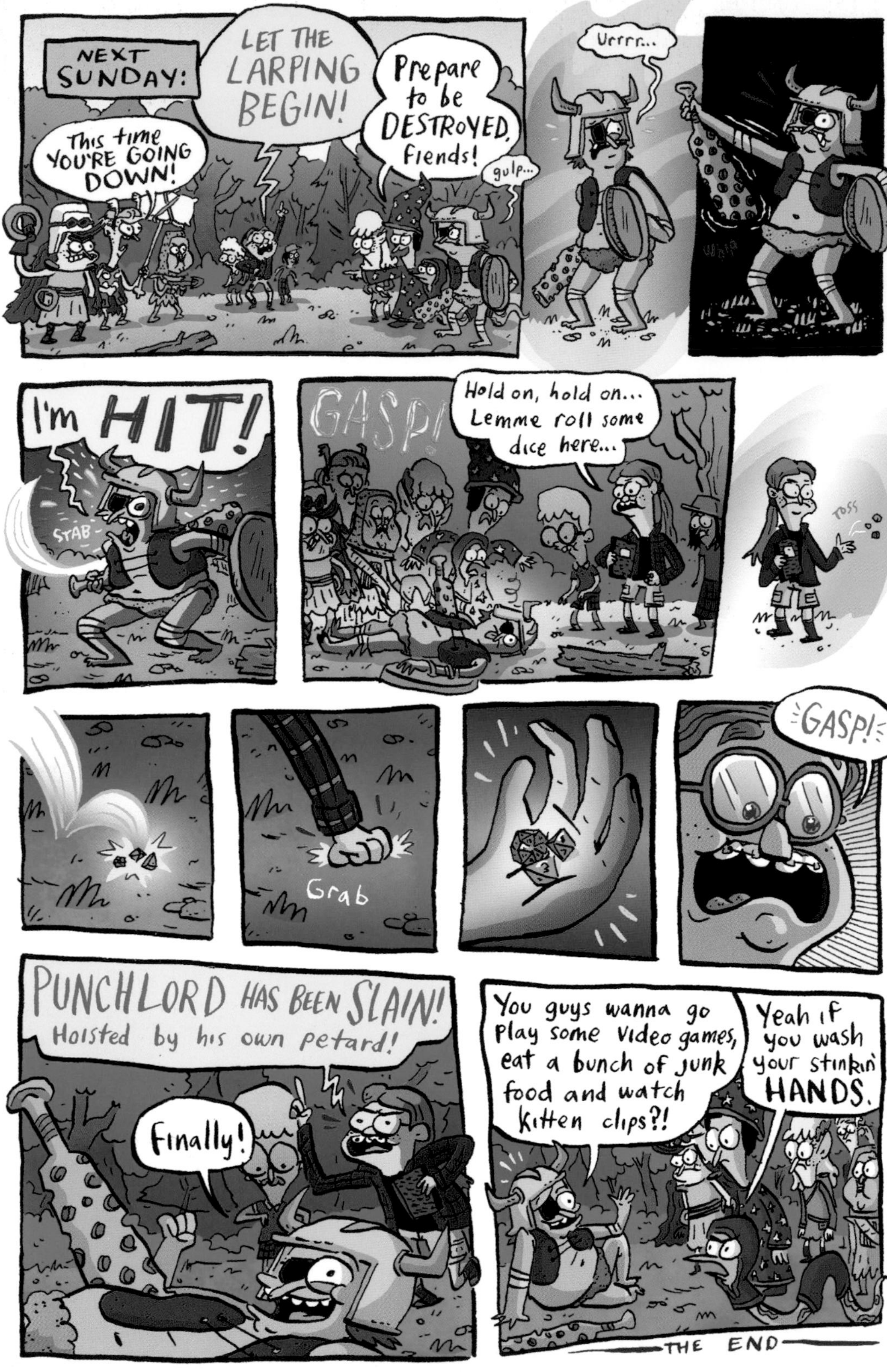
NEXT SUNDAY:
LET THE LARPING BEGIN!
This time YOU'RE GOING DOWN!
Prepare to be DESTROYED, Fiends!
gulp...
Urrrr...
I'm HIT!
STAB
GASP!
Hold on, hold on... Lemme roll some dice here...
TOSS
Grab
GASP!
PUNCHLORD HAS BEEN SLAIN! Hoisted by his own petard!
Finally!
You guys wanna go play some video games, eat a bunch of junk food and watch kitten clips?!
Yeah if you wash your stinkin' HANDS.
THE END

Ever wonder who came up with your favorite NICKELODEON characters? Well, as an extra-special bonus feature for NICKELODEON PANDEMONIUM we're running exclusive behind-the-scenes mini-interviews with the cartoon creators!

DAVE COOPER

Co-creator of . . .

PIG GOAT BANANA CRICKET™

Papercutz: *What inspired you to become a cartoonist?*
Dave Cooper: My parents were friends with a well-known children's book author when I was about 7, Tomi Ungerer. I used to get to watch him draw. Seeing his example, I knew from an early age that it's possible to be an artist as a way of life. I never really considered any other path— it became a foregone conclusion.

A rough sketch inspiring a PGBC episode.

Papercutz: *Did you ever read comics or watch cartoons as a kid? Which were your favorites?*
Dave Cooper: I loved *THE HULK* comics when I was little. *Bugs Bunny* always blew my mind.

Papercutz: *How did you and PGBC co-creator Johnny Ryan meet?*
Dave Cooper: We were both travelling to a big comics festival in France called Angouleme. On the long train ride from Paris to Angouleme we got to know each other. I had been a fan of his work for many years. I thought he'd be a great writer to collaborate with— I've never been good at writing zany comedy, but really wanted to make some funny stories for kids.

PIG GOAT
BANANA CRICKET
HIGH FIVE!

An episode title card for PGBC.

A layout of how the characters interact with their surroundings.

Papercutz: *What got you and Johnny Ryan interested in making PIG GOAT BANANA CRICKET?*
Dave Cooper: It was really the idea of our development executive here at Nickelodeon. She saw a short comic strip we made that starred a pig and a banana. Then, through the development process, we came up with the other characters.

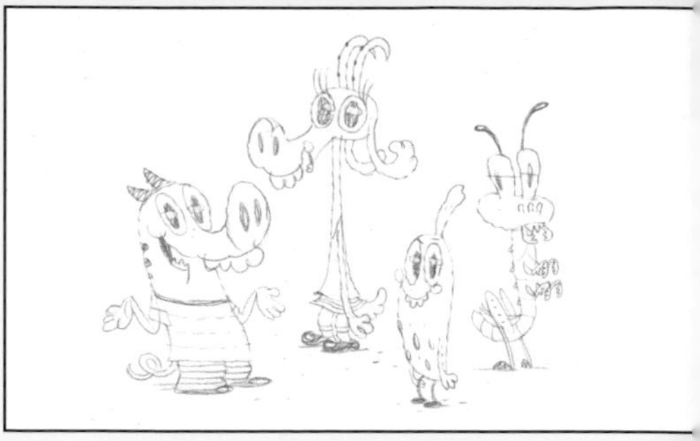

Production sketch of the stars of PGBC.

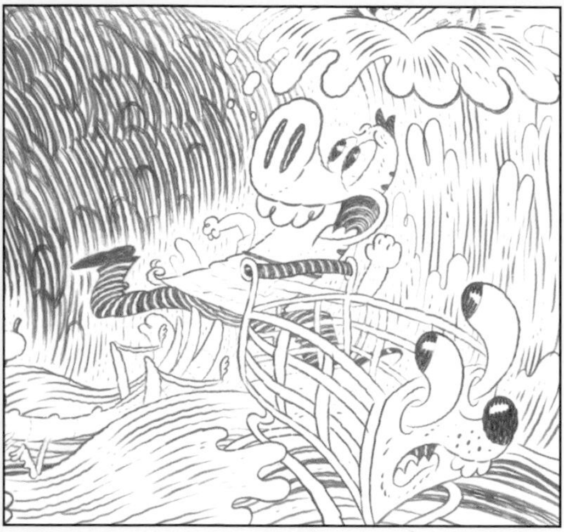

Production sketch of Pig.

Papercutz: *Which character do you relate to the most and why?*
Dave Cooper: Pig. He's not too bright but has a very positive outlook!

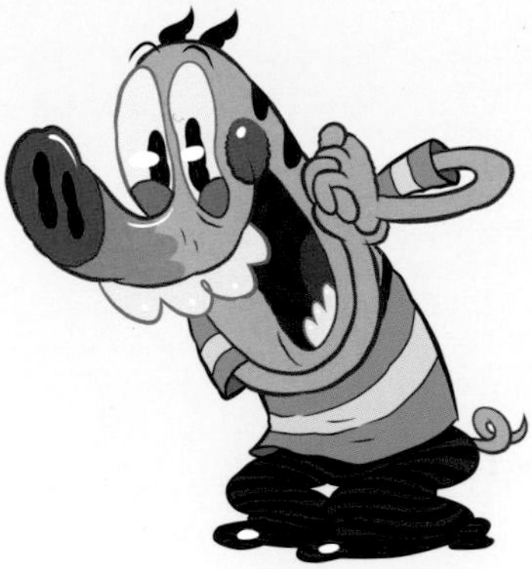

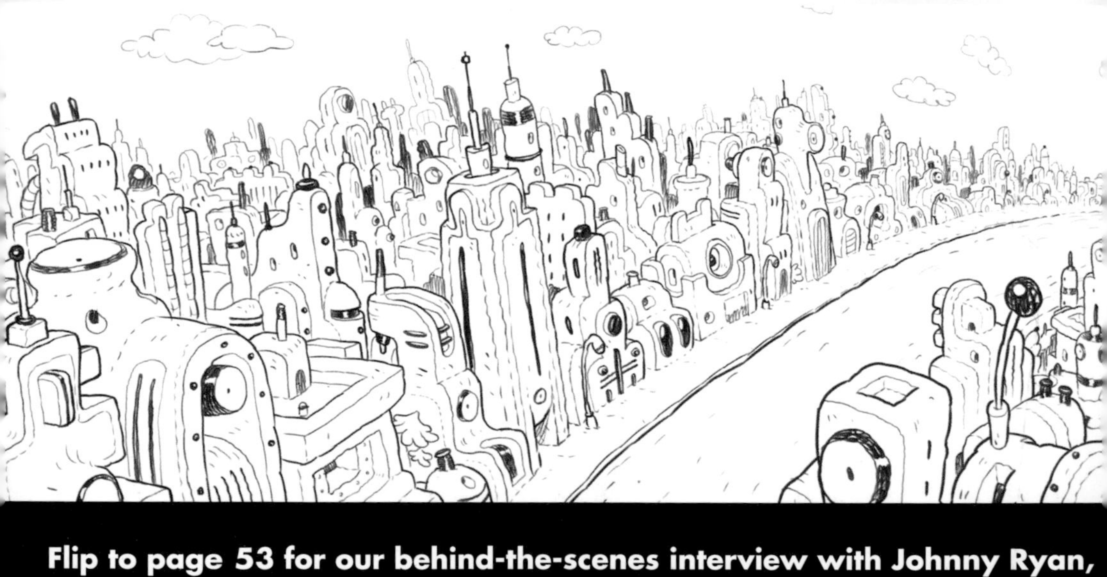

Flip to page 53 for our behind-the-scenes interview with Johnny Ryan, the other co-creator of PIG GOAT BANANA CRICKET!

Summer Treats to Beat The Heat with PIG GOAT BANANA CRICKET

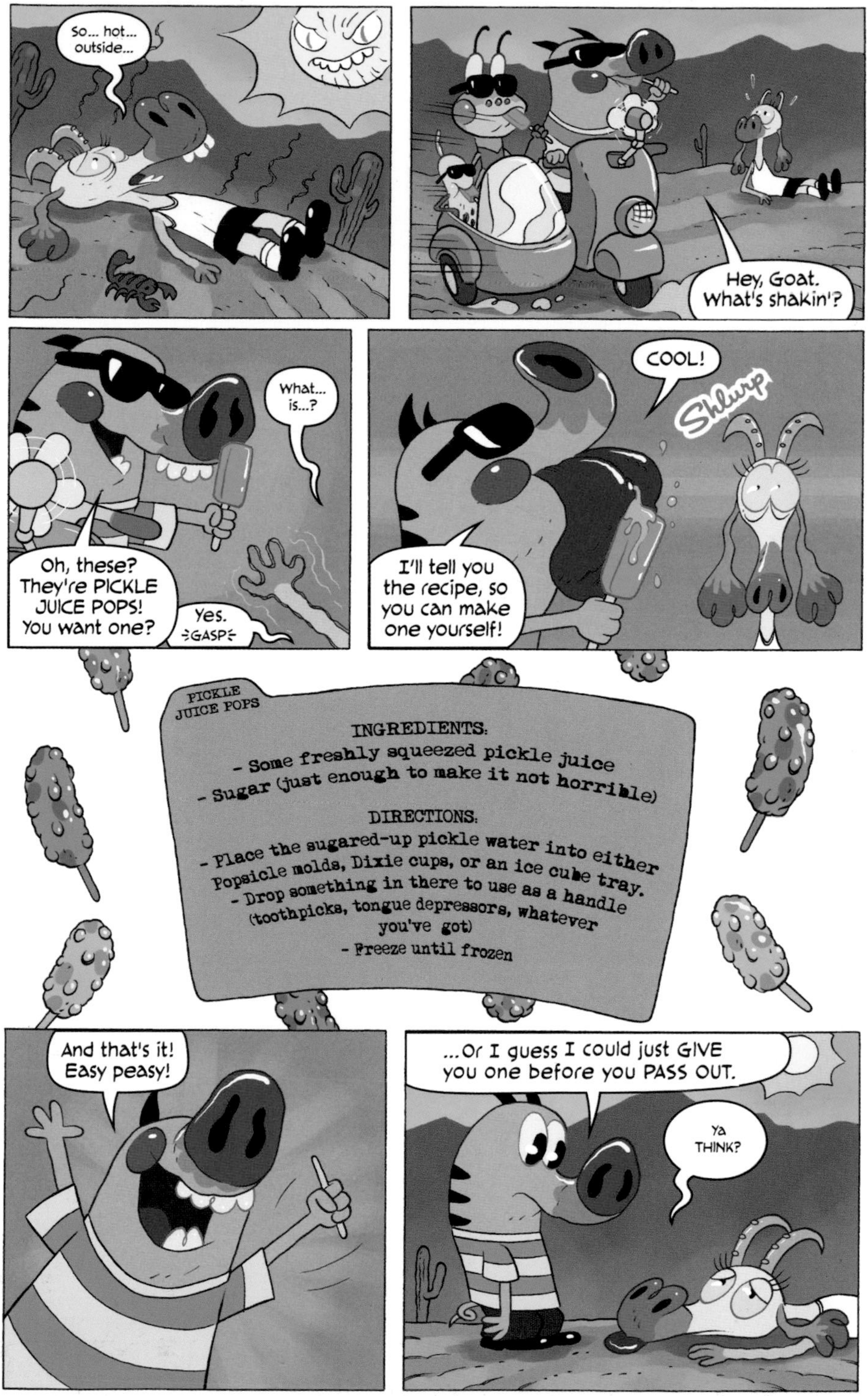
So... hot... outside...
Hey, Goat. What's shakin'?
What... is...?
Oh, these? They're PICKLE JUICE POPS! You want one?
Yes. ≠GASP≠
COOL!
Shlurp
I'll tell you the recipe, so you can make one yourself!
PICKLE JUICE POPS
INGREDIENTS:
- Some freshly squeezed pickle juice
- Sugar (just enough to make it not horrible)
DIRECTIONS:
- Place the sugared-up pickle water into either Popsicle molds, Dixie cups, or an ice cube tray.
- Drop something in there to use as a handle (toothpicks, tongue depressors, whatever you've got)
- Freeze until frozen
And that's it! Easy peasy!
...Or I guess I could just GIVE you one before you PASS OUT.
Ya THINK?

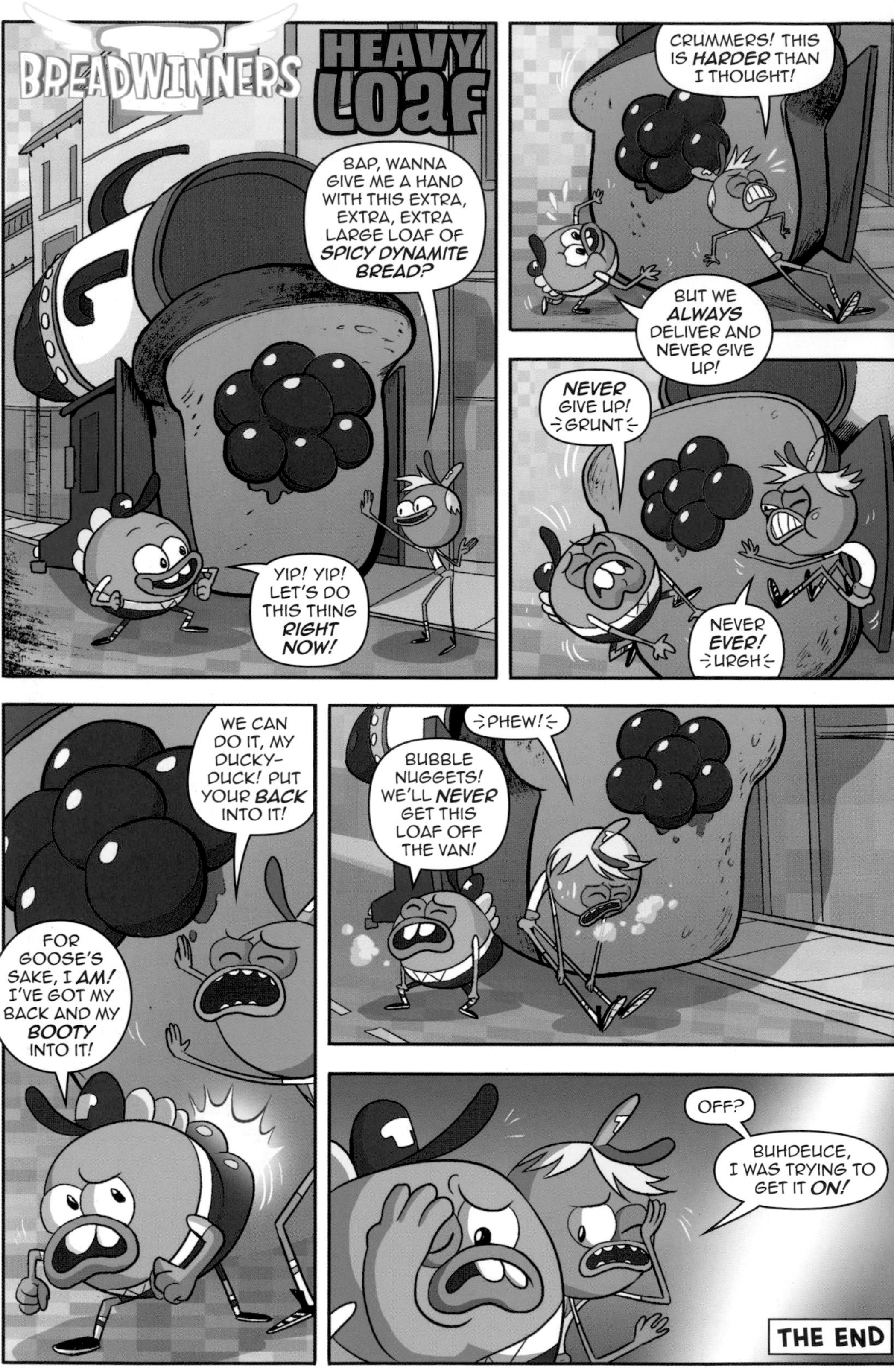
BREADWINNERS
HEAVY LOAF
BAP, WANNA GIVE ME A HAND WITH THIS EXTRA, EXTRA, EXTRA LARGE LOAF OF SPICY DYNAMITE BREAD?
YIP! YIP! LET'S DO THIS THING RIGHT NOW!
CRUMMERS! THIS IS HARDER THAN I THOUGHT!
BUT WE ALWAYS DELIVER AND NEVER GIVE UP!
NEVER GIVE UP! GRUNT
NEVER EVER! URGH
WE CAN DO IT, MY DUCKY-DUCK! PUT YOUR BACK INTO IT!
FOR GOOSE'S SAKE, I AM! I'VE GOT MY BACK AND MY BOOTY INTO IT!
PHEW!
BUBBLE NUGGETS! WE'LL NEVER GET THIS LOAF OFF THE VAN!
OFF?
BUHDEUCE, I WAS TRYING TO GET IT ON!
THE END

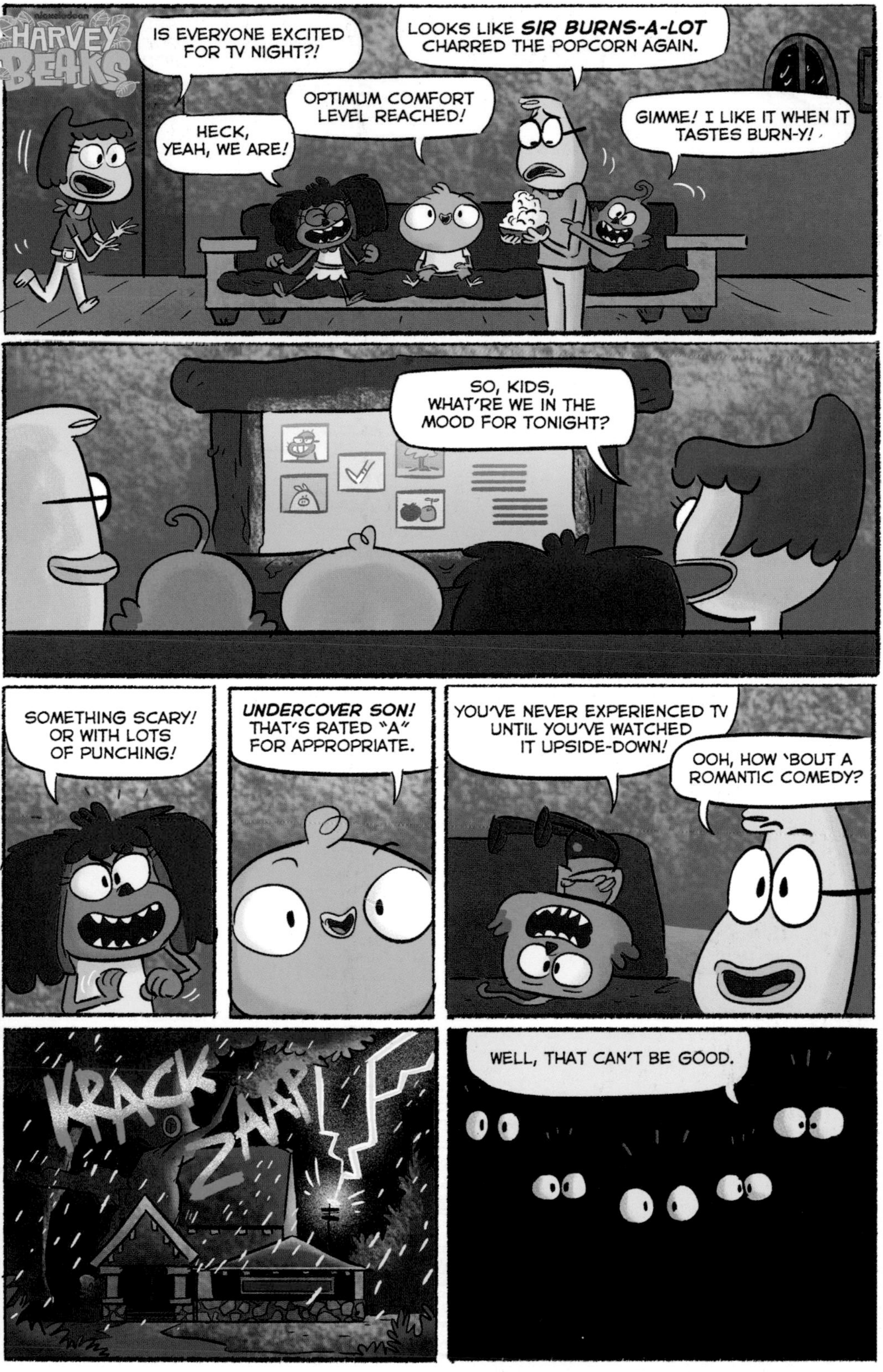

HARVEY BEAKS
IS EVERYONE EXCITED FOR TV NIGHT?!
HECK, YEAH, WE ARE!
OPTIMUM COMFORT LEVEL REACHED!
LOOKS LIKE SIR BURNS-A-LOT CHARRED THE POPCORN AGAIN.
GIMME! I LIKE IT WHEN IT TASTES BURN-Y!
SO, KIDS, WHAT'RE WE IN THE MOOD FOR TONIGHT?
SOMETHING SCARY! OR WITH LOTS OF PUNCHING!
UNDERCOVER SON! THAT'S RATED "A" FOR APPROPRIATE.
YOU'VE NEVER EXPERIENCED TV UNTIL YOU'VE WATCHED IT UPSIDE-DOWN!
OOH, HOW 'BOUT A ROMANTIC COMEDY?
KRACK
ZAAP!
WELL, THAT CAN'T BE GOOD.

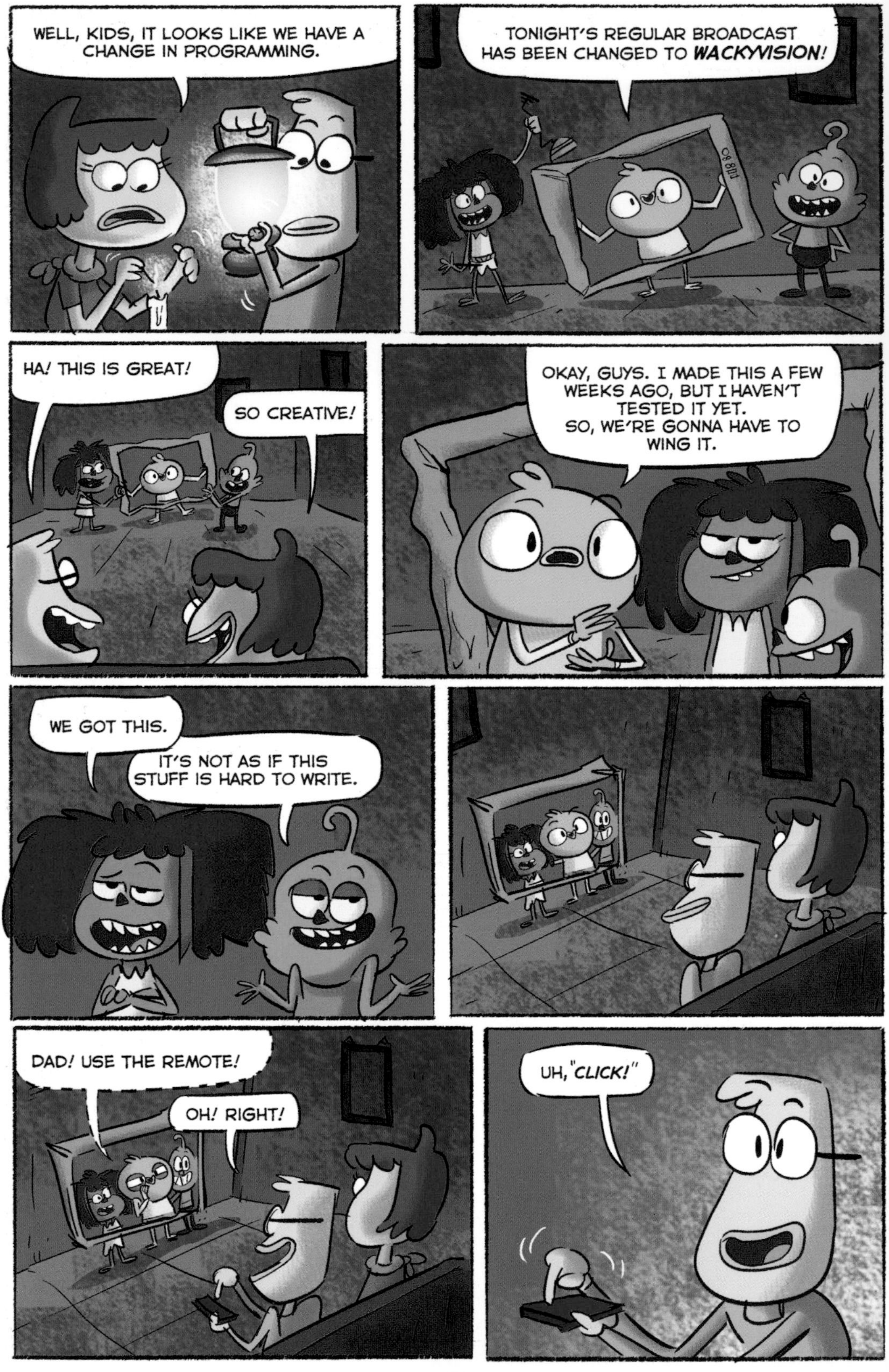

WELL, KIDS, IT LOOKS LIKE WE HAVE A CHANGE IN PROGRAMMING.
TONIGHT'S REGULAR BROADCAST HAS BEEN CHANGED TO ***WACKYVISION***!
HA! THIS IS GREAT!
SO CREATIVE!
OKAY, GUYS. I MADE THIS A FEW WEEKS AGO, BUT I HAVEN'T TESTED IT YET. SO, WE'RE GONNA HAVE TO WING IT.
WE GOT THIS.
IT'S NOT AS IF THIS STUFF IS HARD TO WRITE.
DAD! USE THE REMOTE!
OH! RIGHT!
UH, "***CLICK!***"

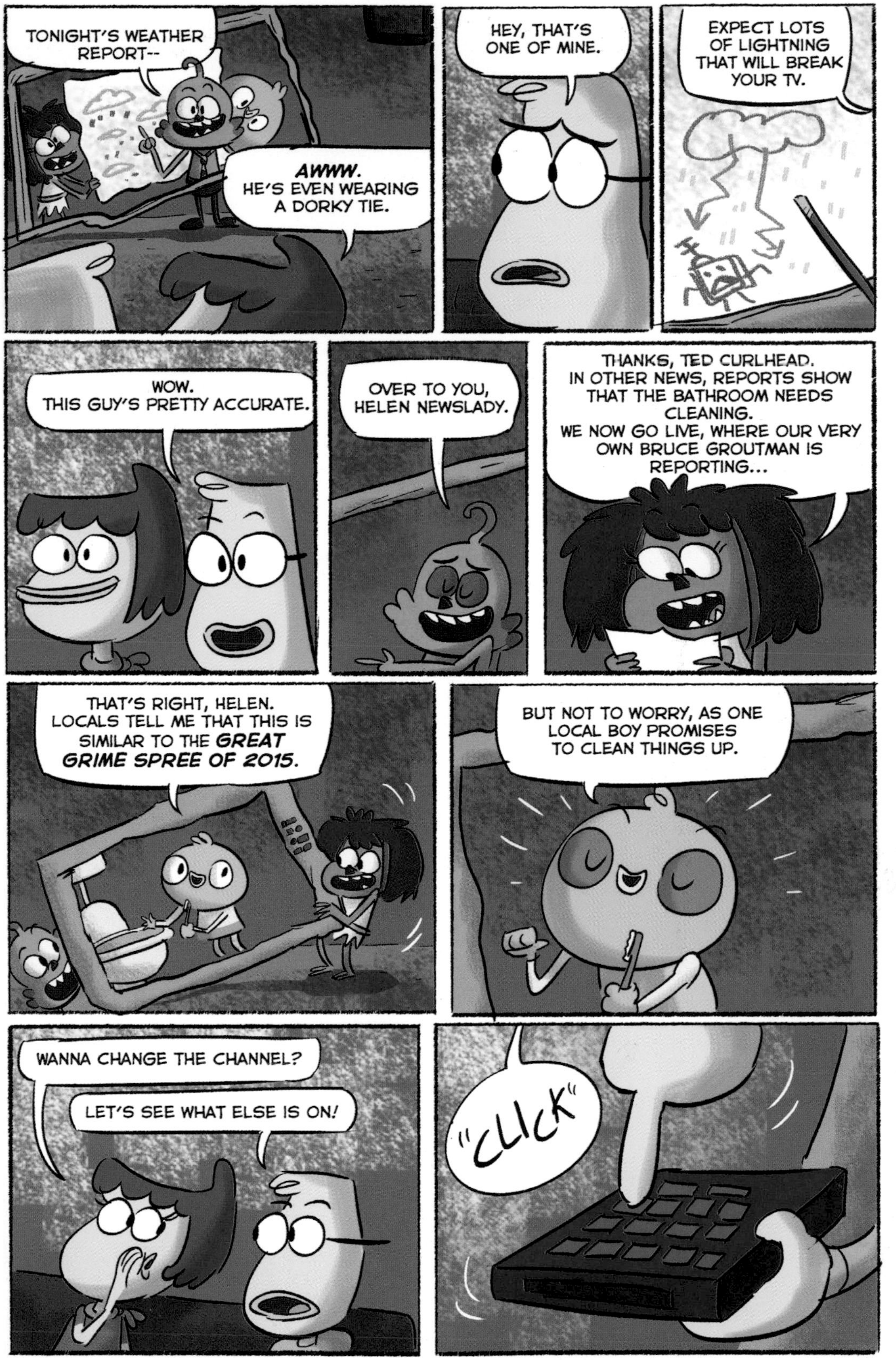
TONIGHT'S WEATHER REPORT--
AWWW. HE'S EVEN WEARING A DORKY TIE.
HEY, THAT'S ONE OF MINE.
EXPECT LOTS OF LIGHTNING THAT WILL BREAK YOUR TV.
WOW. THIS GUY'S PRETTY ACCURATE.
OVER TO YOU, HELEN NEWSLADY.
THANKS, TED CURLHEAD. IN OTHER NEWS, REPORTS SHOW THAT THE BATHROOM NEEDS CLEANING. WE NOW GO LIVE, WHERE OUR VERY OWN BRUCE GROUTMAN IS REPORTING...
THAT'S RIGHT, HELEN. LOCALS TELL ME THAT THIS IS SIMILAR TO THE GREAT GRIME SPREE OF 2015.
BUT NOT TO WORRY, AS ONE LOCAL BOY PROMISES TO CLEAN THINGS UP.
WANNA CHANGE THE CHANNEL?
LET'S SEE WHAT ELSE IS ON!
"CLICK"

WELCOME TO **COOKING WITH HARVEY!**

TONIGHT, WE LEARN HOW TO MAKE THAT DIFFICULT DISH WE ALL LOVE...**TOAST!**

TAKE NOTE, **SIR BURNS-A-LOT.**

IT'S NOT **MY** FAULT. I'M PRETTY SURE THE TOASTER IS BROKEN.

FIRST, INSERT TWO SLICES OF BREAD. I WAS FEELING A BIT WHIMSICAL, SO I DECIDED TO GO WITH PUMPERNICKEL TODAY.

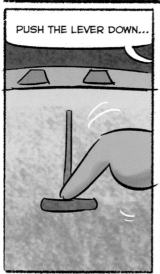

PUSH THE LEVER DOWN...

TURN THE DIAL TO IDEAL TOASTING PREFERENCE. I ENJOY MINE **SLIGHTLY TOASTED,** SO I'M GOING WITH 3 ½.

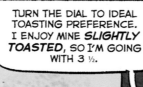

WAIT. THERE'S A **DIAL**?!

THAT EXPLAINS EVERYTHING.

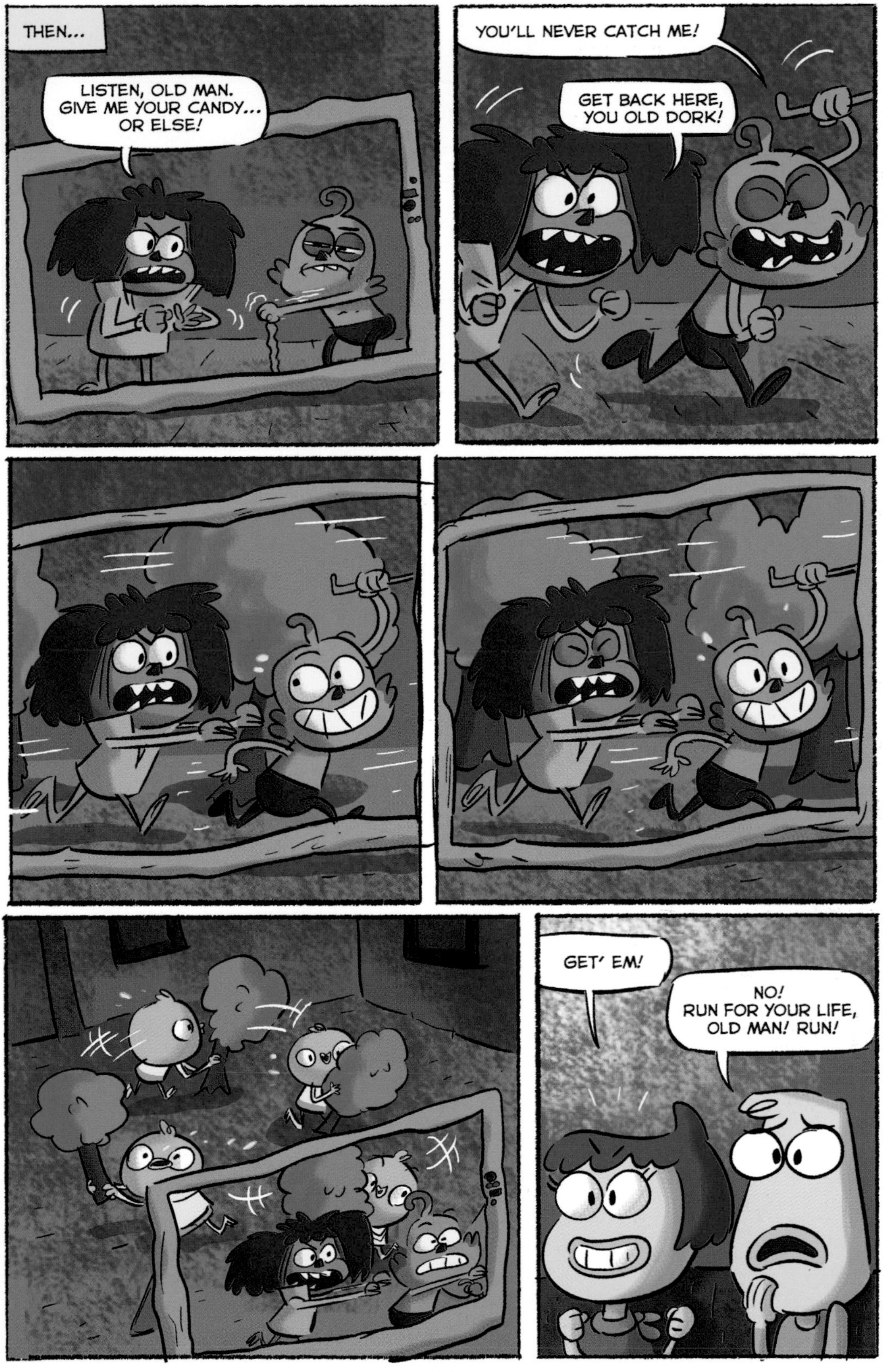
THEN...
LISTEN, OLD MAN. GIVE ME YOUR CANDY... OR ELSE!
YOU'LL NEVER CATCH ME!
GET BACK HERE, YOU OLD DORK!
GET' EM!
NO! RUN FOR YOUR LIFE, OLD MAN! RUN!

THEN...

WELCOME TO LITTLEBARK'S FAVORITE GAME SHOW, *CAN YOU PUNCH THAT?*

CLAP CLAP CLAP

CONTESTANT NUMBER 1. CAN YOU PUNCH THAT?

HMMMM?

VEGGIE CHIPS

YES!

CORRECT! YOU *CAN* PUNCH THAT!

VEGGIE CHIPS

KABUM

CONTESTANT NUMBER 2. CAN YOU PUNCH THAT?

UH. NO?

WRONG! YOU *CAN* PUNCH THAT!

KASPLOIZ

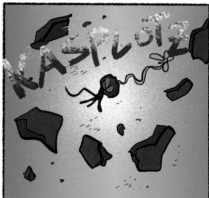

QUICK, MIRIAM! CHANGE THE CHANNEL!

"CLICK"

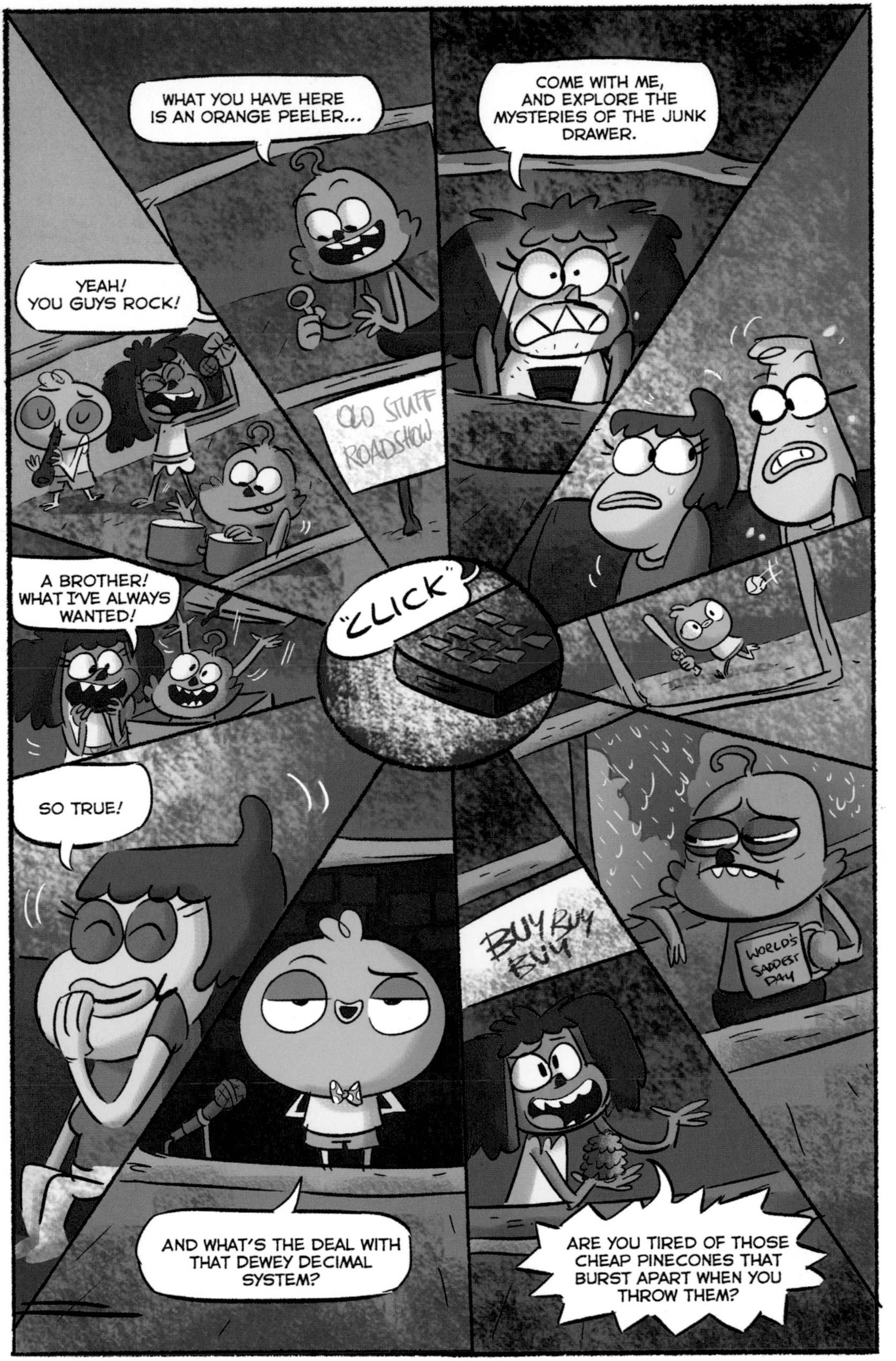

WHAT YOU HAVE HERE IS AN ORANGE PEELER...
COME WITH ME, AND EXPLORE THE MYSTERIES OF THE JUNK DRAWER.
YEAH! YOU GUYS ROCK!
OLD STUFF ROADSHOW
A BROTHER! WHAT I'VE ALWAYS WANTED!
"CLICK"
SO TRUE!
BUY BUY BUY
WORLD'S SADDEST DAY
AND WHAT'S THE DEAL WITH THAT DEWEY DECIMAL SYSTEM?
ARE YOU TIRED OF THOSE CHEAP PINECONES THAT BURST APART WHEN YOU THROW THEM?

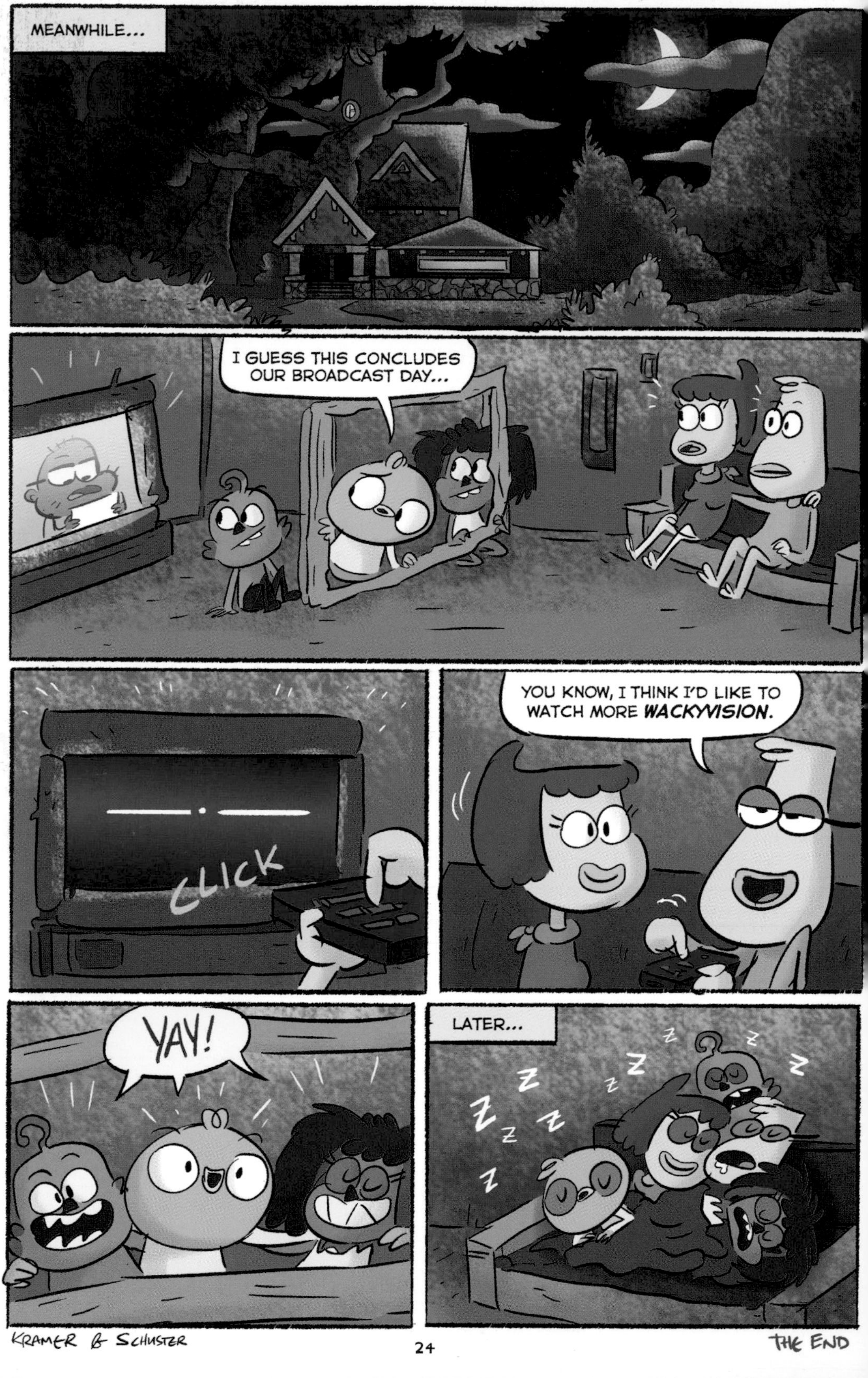
MEANWHILE...
I GUESS THIS CONCLUDES OUR BROADCAST DAY...
CLICK
YOU KNOW, I THINK I'D LIKE TO WATCH MORE WACKYVISION.
YAY!
LATER...
Z Z Z
KRAMER & SCHUSTER
THE END

NICKELODEON PANDEMONIUM continues to give you an extra-special behind-the-scenes look at the creators of your favorite NICKELODEON shows! How were Harvey Beaks and his friends created?

Let's talk to:

C.H. GREENBLATT

Creator of . . .

nickelodeon HARVEY BEAKS

Papercutz: *What made you interested in creating cartoons?*
C.H. Greenblatt: I love that you create anything you imagine. You can be super silly and do all the things you can't do in real life. Plus I really like making people laugh.

Papercutz: *Did you watch any cartoons or read any comics as a kid? If so what were your favorites?*
C.H. Greenblatt: I watched EVERYTHING but I especially loved *The Muppets, Looney Tunes, G.I. Joe, X-Men,* and *Spider-Man.* Some of the comics I read were *The Far Side, Calvin & Hobbes, Garfield,* and *Bloom County.*

An early design of Harvey, Fee, and Foo.

Papercutz: *When did you first get started in animation?*
C.H. Greenblatt: My first job was on *SpongeBob SquarePants* as a storyboard revisionist. That means I helped make technical fixes to the storyboards. The best part of that job is you get to work on all the episodes and learn a lot from each different artist.

Harvey should always be dimensional and not flatten out.
His eyes should be set apart wide. They can move and change size as needed for expression.
His head is oval but should be imperfect and irregular.
His body, arms, shorts, & legs are cylinders. His mouth always starts between his eyes.
His hands are usually small, but can grow if needed.
His arms can stretch.

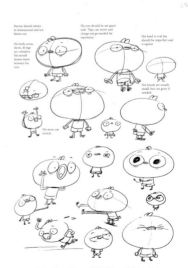

Model sheet for Harvey Beaks.

Papercutz: *What was the concept behind making HARVEY BEAKS?*
C.H. Greenblatt: I wanted it to be about an unlikely friendship. Harvey was a kid much like myself. He didn't do anything too crazy, but he still had fun and enjoyed himself. His friends, Fee and Foo, were like some of my friends. They were wilder than me, but we got along because we respected each other. Sometimes, I'd be uncomfortable but I still always had fun. Harvey gets pushed outside his comfort zone by his friends and learns to grow. Fee and Foo get a sense of belonging with Harvey because he accepts them as they are. This was a relationship I felt was really strong for storytelling.

Papercutz: *How do you come up with your stories?*
C.H. Greenblatt: The writers and I spend a lot of time talking about our childhood. We think about the things that excited us or scared us or made us laugh and start building stories from there.

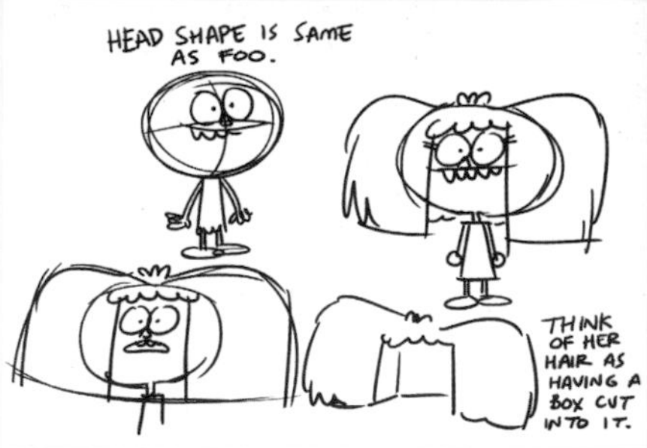
HEAD SHAPE IS SAME AS FOO.
THINK OF HER HAIR AS HAVING A BOX CUT INTO IT.
Did you know that Fee and Foo have the same head shape?

Papercutz: *How did you create the concepts behind the characters themselves?*
C.H. Greenblatt: I try to think of distinct personalities that everyone can relate to. Sometimes it starts with someone you know. Then you think of how that character interacts with other characters in the series and ask if it's funny or interesting.

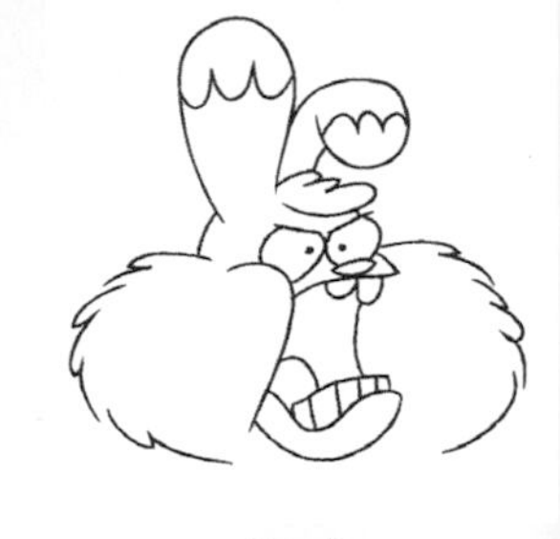
Dade

Papercutz: *Which character is your favorite and why?*
C.H. Greenblatt: Dade is the most fun to write because he gets overly emotional so easily. I also like him because I get to do his voice!

Papercutz: *Which character do you relate to the most and why?*
C.H. Greenblatt: I'm the most like Harvey. I'm very neat and follow all the rules. I also like being nice to people and generally avoid getting into any trouble.

Papercutz: *What would you do if you ever got to hang out with Harvey, Fee, and Foo?*
C.H. Greenblatt: We'd get out some extreme label-makers and organize the forest!

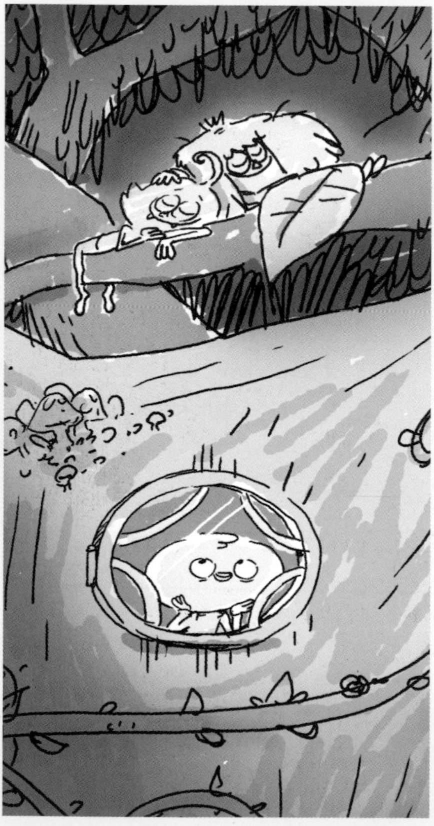
A production sketch from a Harvey Beaks scene.

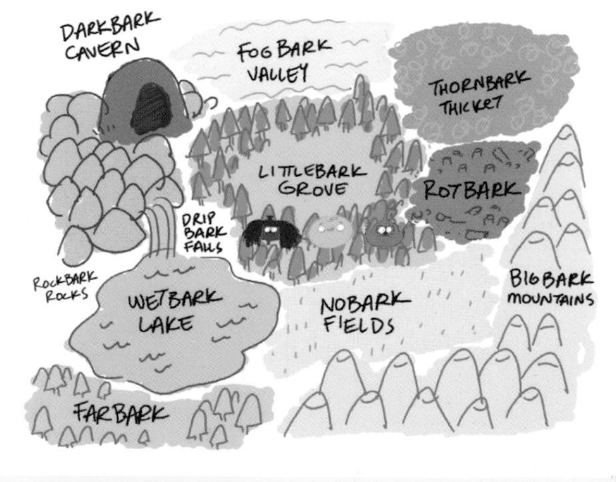
DARKBARK CAVERN
FOG BARK VALLEY
THORNBARK THICKET
LITTLEBARK GROVE
ROTBARK
DRIP BARK FALLS
ROCKBARK ROCKS
WETBARK LAKE
NOBARK FIELDS
BIGBARK MOUNTAINS
FARBARK
A map used by the Harvey Beaks production team.

CRICKET'S SCIENCE CORNER

It's snowing SPRINKLES on top of that ol' ICE CREAM mountain, and--

Aww, DANG! I broke the string from ROCKIN' too hard!

SNAP

Flib flabbin' flibble flubbin--PHOEEY! I was really in a mood to BOOGIE!

Silly Goat! You don't need an instrument to play music!

I don't?

Heck, naw!

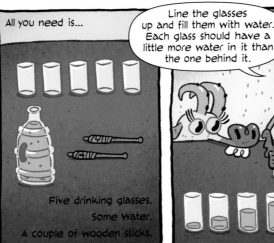

All you need is...

Five drinking glasses.
Some Water.
A couple of wooden sticks.

Line the glasses up and fill them with water. Each glass should have a little more water in it than the one behind it.

Now experiment with tapping your stick against the cups. Hear that sound?

The cup with the most water should have the lowest tone.

--And the cup with the least water has the highest! WHOA!

Hit the other glasses and see what noise they make! Try to write a song using the different tones!

That's CRAZY!

Be straight with me, Cricket... is this the work of BLACK MAGICK?

Even cooler! It's science!

Tiny vibrations are made when you drum on the glass, which creates sound waves that travel through the water!

More water means slower vibrations, and slower vibrations means a deeper tone.

Neat!

END.

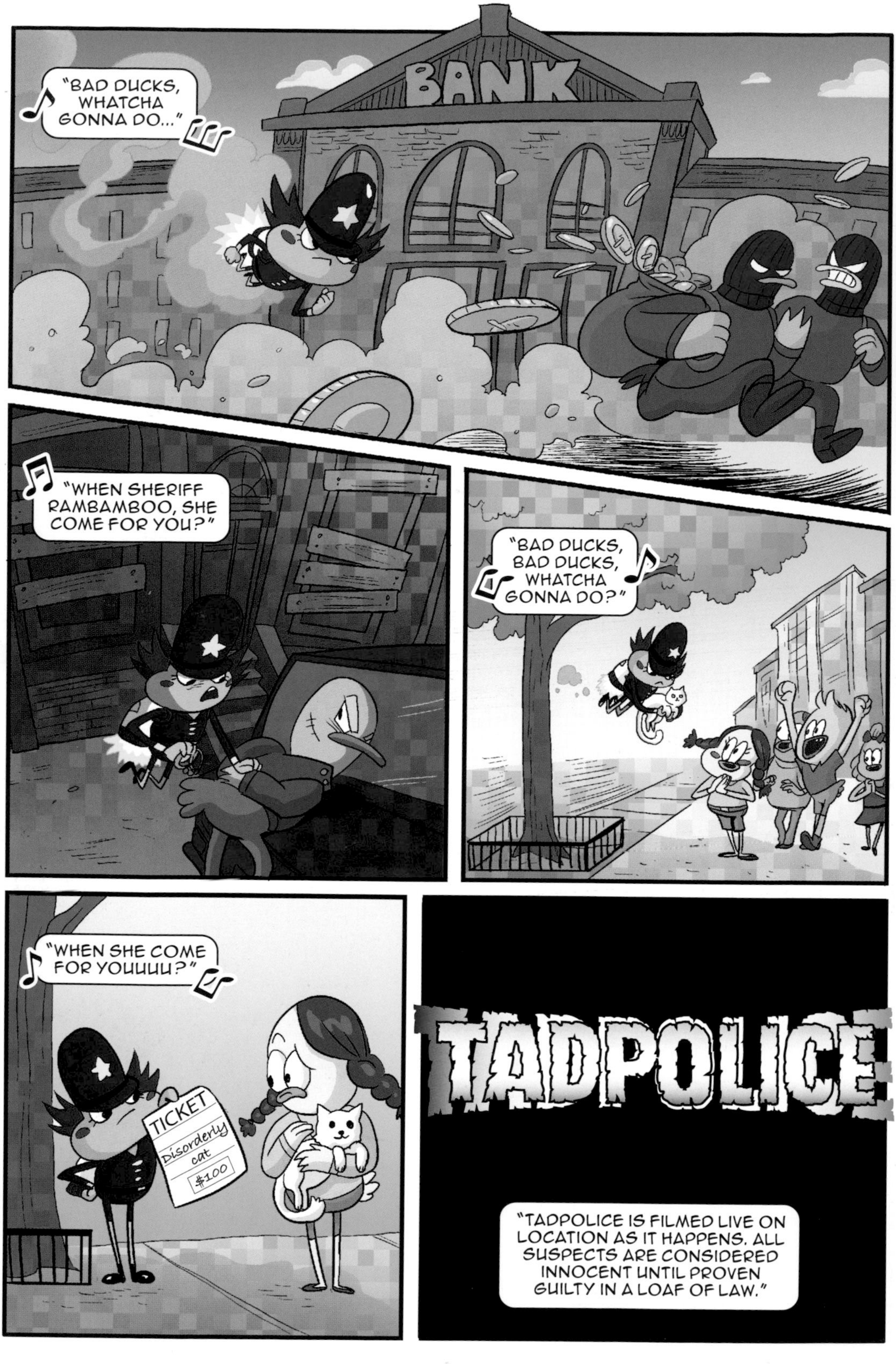
BANK
"BAD DUCKS, WHATCHA GONNA DO..."
"WHEN SHERIFF RAMBAMBOO, SHE COME FOR YOU?"
"BAD DUCKS, BAD DUCKS, WHATCHA GONNA DO?"
"WHEN SHE COME FOR YOUUUU?"
TICKET
Disorderly cat
$100
TADPOLICE
"TADPOLICE IS FILMED LIVE ON LOCATION AS IT HAPPENS. ALL SUSPECTS ARE CONSIDERED INNOCENT UNTIL PROVEN GUILTY IN A LOAF OF LAW."

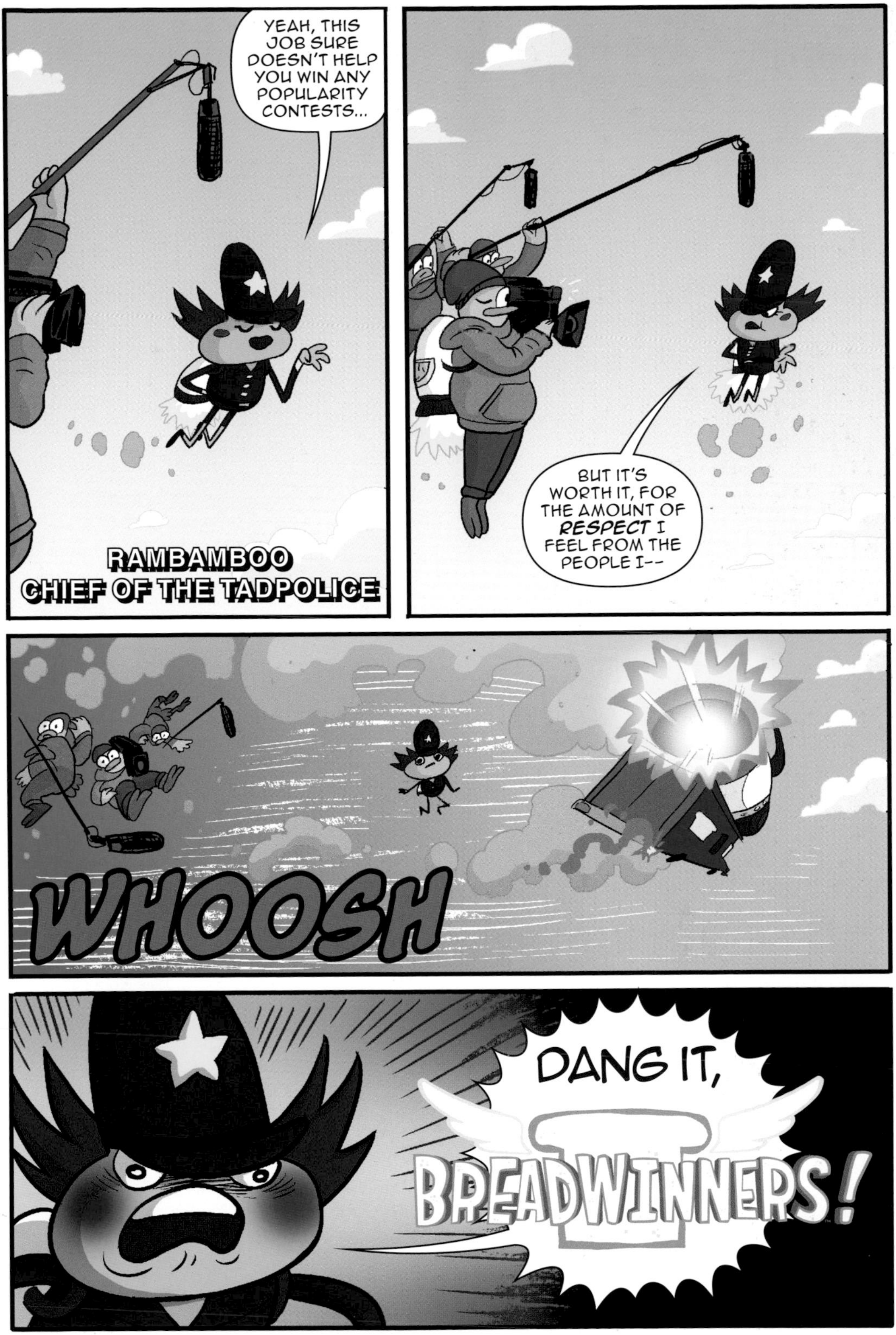
YEAH, THIS JOB SURE DOESN'T HELP YOU WIN ANY POPULARITY CONTESTS...
RAMBAMBOO
CHIEF OF THE TADPOLICE
BUT IT'S WORTH IT, FOR THE AMOUNT OF RESPECT I FEEL FROM THE PEOPLE I--
WHOOSH
DANG IT,
BREADWINNERS!

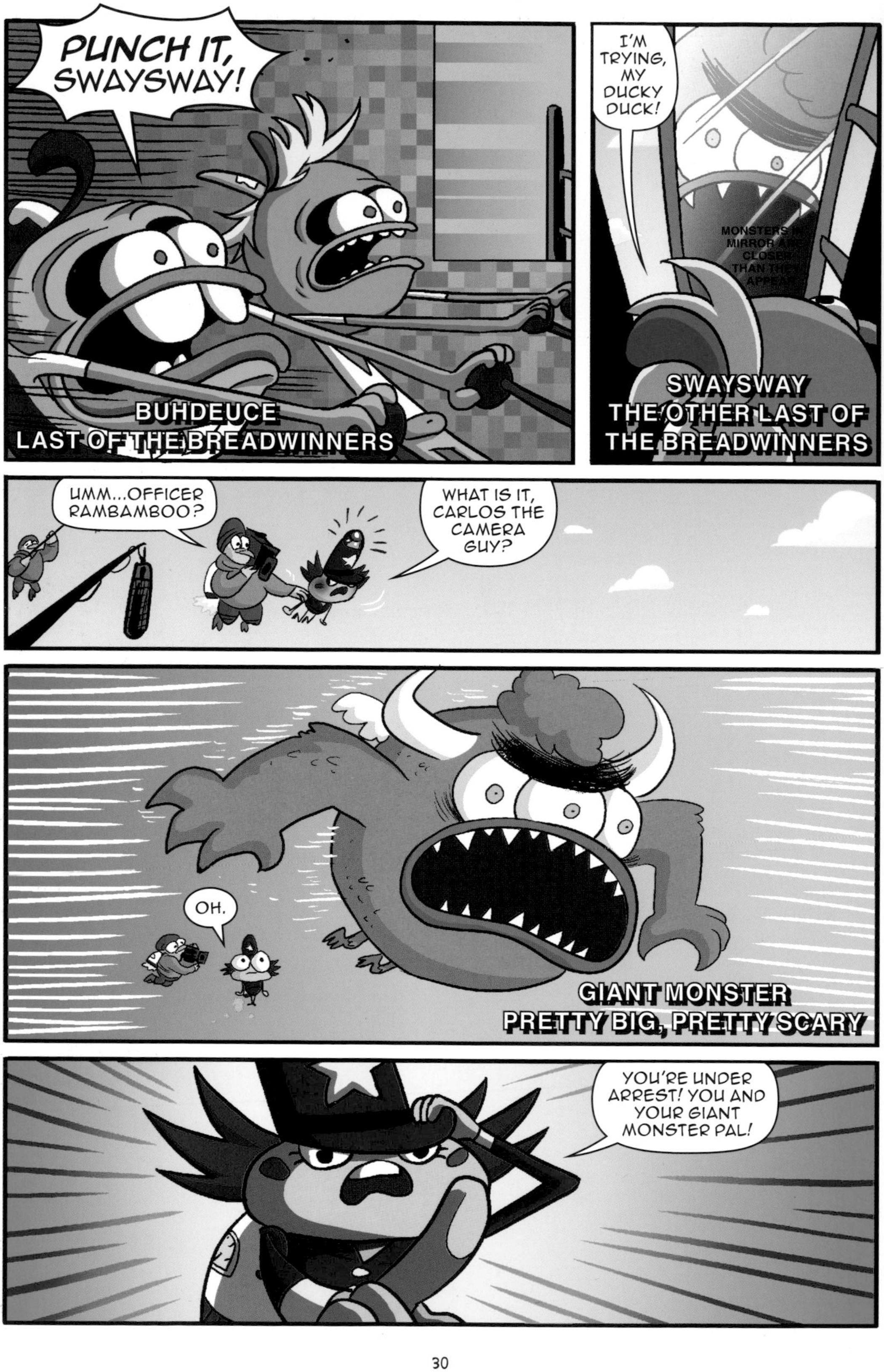
PUNCH IT, SWAYSWAY!
BUHDEUCE
LAST OF THE BREADWINNERS
I'M TRYING, MY DUCKY DUCK!
SWAYSWAY
THE OTHER LAST OF THE BREADWINNERS
UMM...OFFICER RAMBAMBOO?
WHAT IS IT, CARLOS THE CAMERA GUY?
OH.
GIANT MONSTER
PRETTY BIG, PRETTY SCARY
YOU'RE UNDER ARREST! YOU AND YOUR GIANT MONSTER PAL!

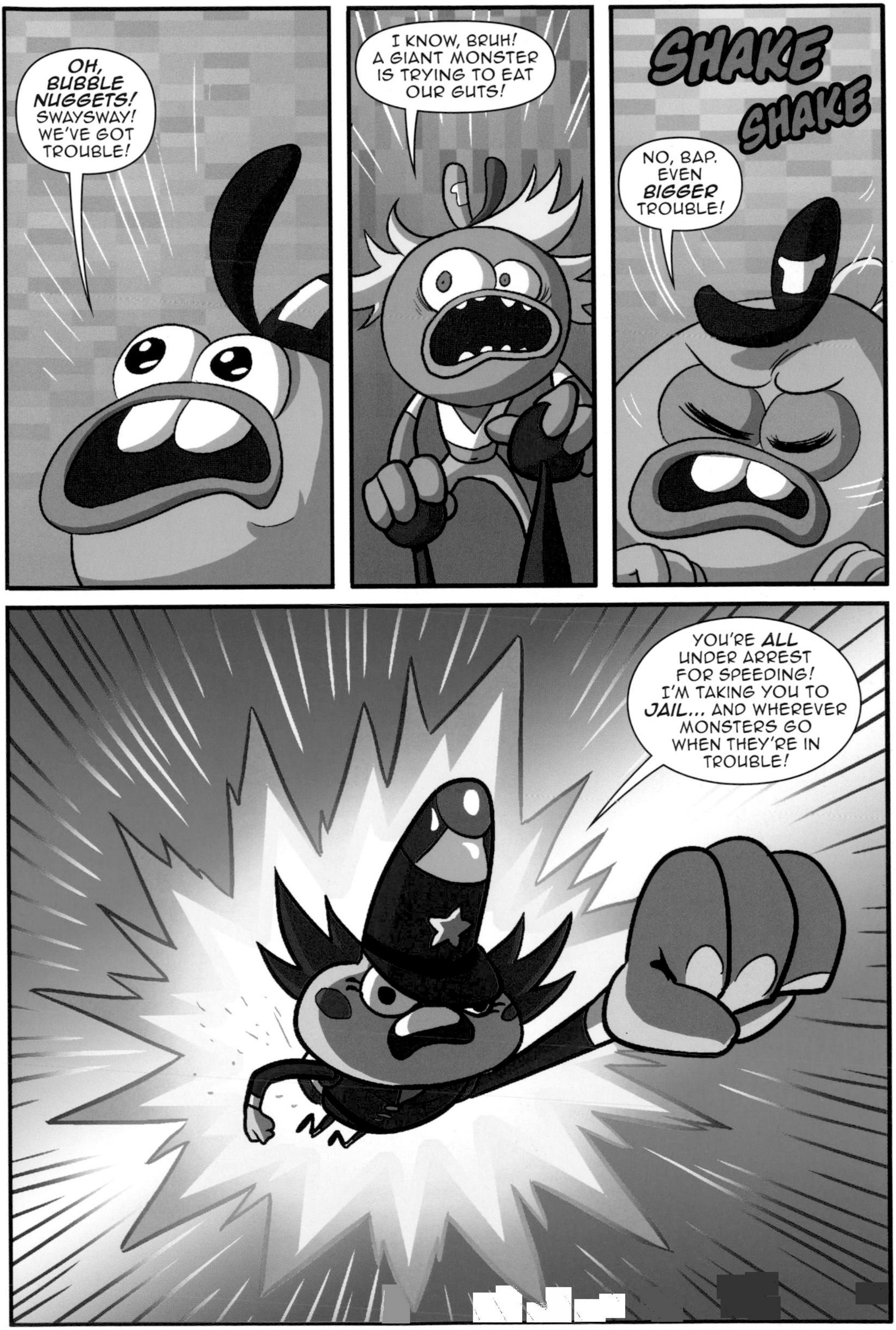
OH, BUBBLE NUGGETS! SWAYSWAY! WE'VE GOT TROUBLE!
I KNOW, BRUH! A GIANT MONSTER IS TRYING TO EAT OUR GUTS!
SHAKE
SHAKE
NO, BAP. EVEN BIGGER TROUBLE!
YOU'RE ALL UNDER ARREST FOR SPEEDING! I'M TAKING YOU TO JAIL... AND WHEREVER MONSTERS GO WHEN THEY'RE IN TROUBLE!

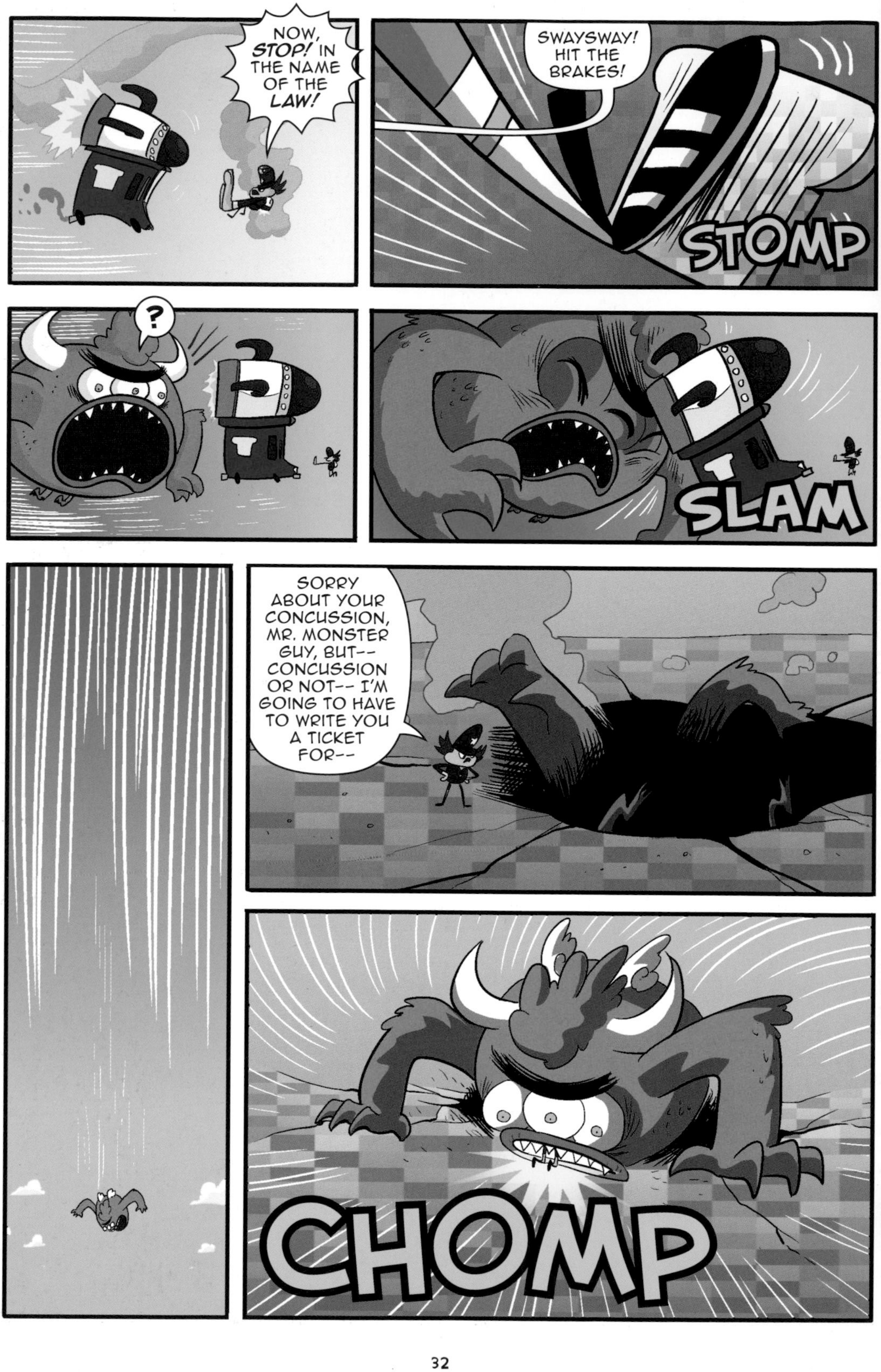
NOW, STOP! IN THE NAME OF THE LAW!
SWAYSWAY! HIT THE BRAKES!
STOMP
?
SLAM
SORRY ABOUT YOUR CONCUSSION, MR. MONSTER GUY, BUT-- CONCUSSION OR NOT-- I'M GOING TO HAVE TO WRITE YOU A TICKET FOR--
CHOMP

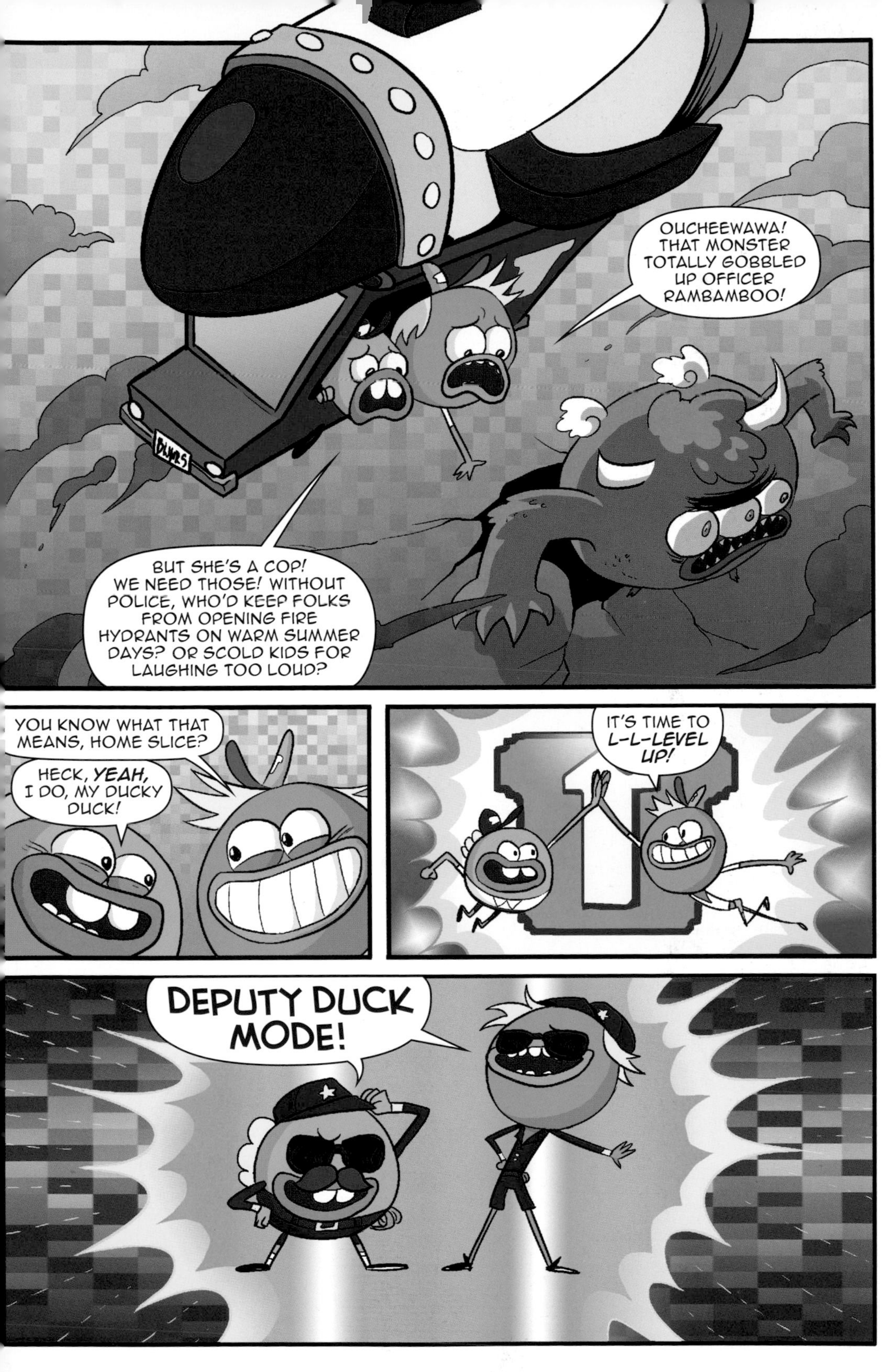
OUCHEEWAWA! THAT MONSTER TOTALLY GOBBLED UP OFFICER RAMBAMBOO!
BUT SHE'S A COP! WE NEED THOSE! WITHOUT POLICE, WHO'D KEEP FOLKS FROM OPENING FIRE HYDRANTS ON WARM SUMMER DAYS? OR SCOLD KIDS FOR LAUGHING TOO LOUD?
YOU KNOW WHAT THAT MEANS, HOME SLICE?
HECK, *YEAH,* I DO, MY DUCKY DUCK!
IT'S TIME TO *L-L-LEVEL UP!*
DEPUTY DUCK MODE!

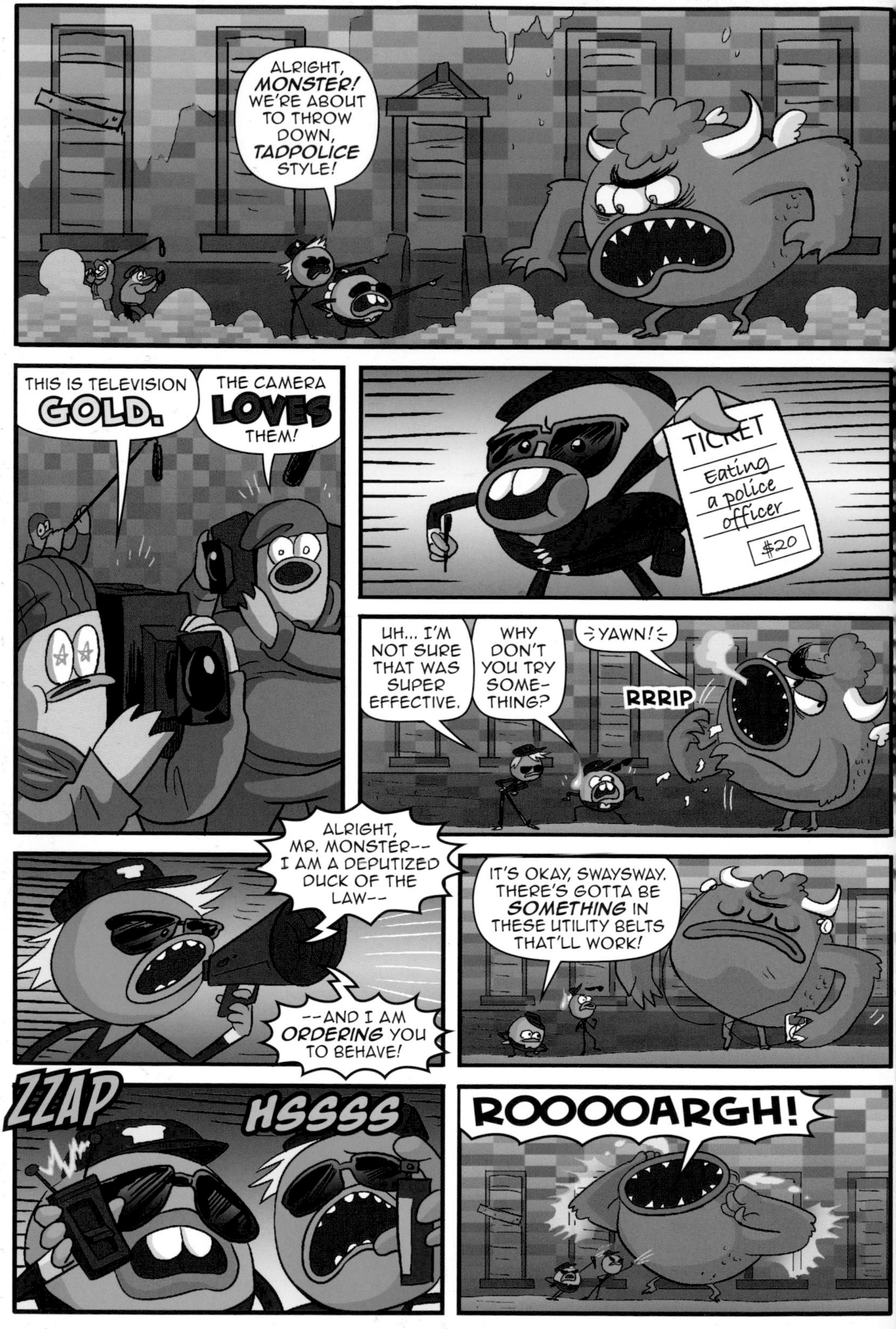
ALRIGHT, MONSTER! WE'RE ABOUT TO THROW DOWN, TADPOLICE STYLE!
THIS IS TELEVISION GOLD.
THE CAMERA LOVES THEM!
TICKET
Eating a police officer
$20
UH... I'M NOT SURE THAT WAS SUPER EFFECTIVE.
WHY DON'T YOU TRY SOME-THING?
YAWN!
RRRIP
ALRIGHT, MR. MONSTER-- I AM A DEPUTIZED DUCK OF THE LAW--
--AND I AM ORDERING YOU TO BEHAVE!
IT'S OKAY, SWAYSWAY. THERE'S GOTTA BE SOMETHING IN THESE UTILITY BELTS THAT'LL WORK!
ZZAP
HSSSS
ROOOOARGH!

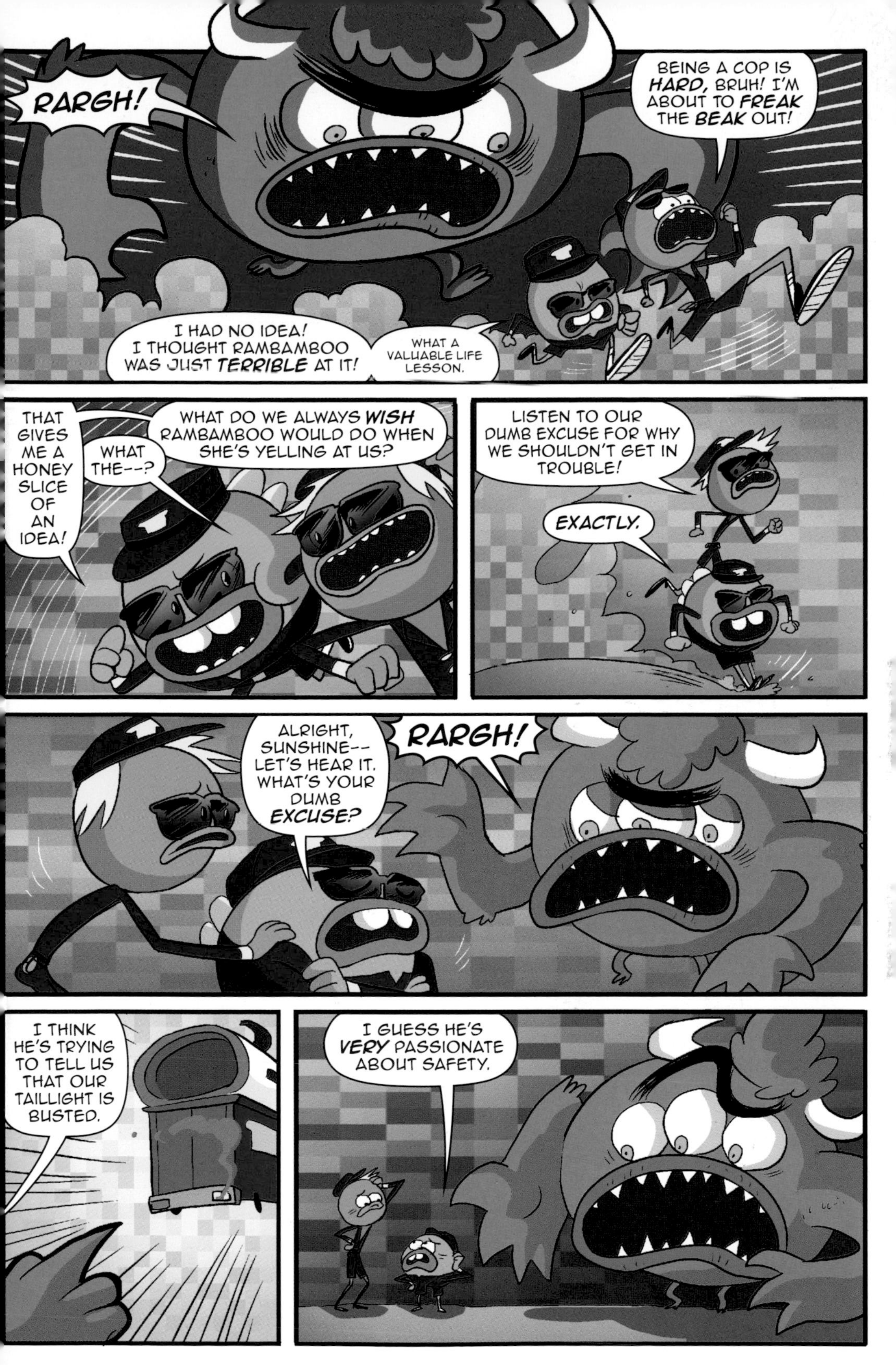
RARGH!
BEING A COP IS HARD, BRUH! I'M ABOUT TO FREAK THE BEAK OUT!
I HAD NO IDEA! I THOUGHT RAMBAMBOO WAS JUST TERRIBLE AT IT!
WHAT A VALUABLE LIFE LESSON.
THAT GIVES ME A HONEY SLICE OF AN IDEA!
WHAT THE--?
WHAT DO WE ALWAYS WISH RAMBAMBOO WOULD DO WHEN SHE'S YELLING AT US?
LISTEN TO OUR DUMB EXCUSE FOR WHY WE SHOULDN'T GET IN TROUBLE!
EXACTLY.
ALRIGHT, SUNSHINE-- LET'S HEAR IT. WHAT'S YOUR DUMB EXCUSE?
RARGH!
I THINK HE'S TRYING TO TELL US THAT OUR TAILLIGHT IS BUSTED.
I GUESS HE'S VERY PASSIONATE ABOUT SAFETY.

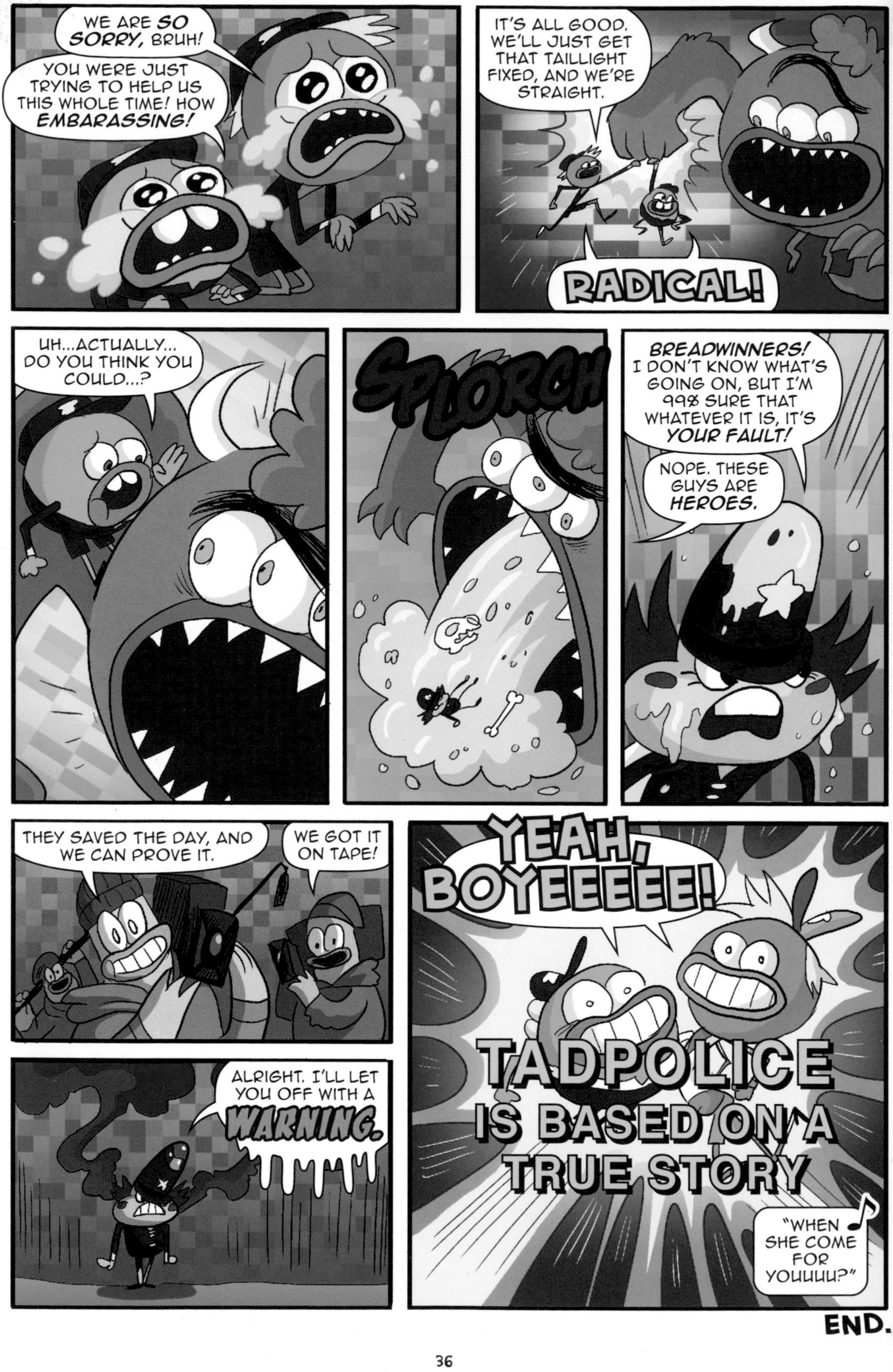
WE ARE SO SORRY, BRUH!
YOU WERE JUST TRYING TO HELP US THIS WHOLE TIME! HOW EMBARASSING!
IT'S ALL GOOD. WE'LL JUST GET THAT TAILLIGHT FIXED, AND WE'RE STRAIGHT.
RADICAL!
UH...ACTUALLY... DO YOU THINK YOU COULD...?
SPLORCH
BREADWINNERS! I DON'T KNOW WHAT'S GOING ON, BUT I'M 99% SURE THAT WHATEVER IT IS, IT'S YOUR FAULT!
NOPE. THESE GUYS ARE HEROES.
THEY SAVED THE DAY, AND WE CAN PROVE IT.
WE GOT IT ON TAPE!
ALRIGHT. I'LL LET YOU OFF WITH A WARNING.
YEAH, BOYEEEEE!
TADPOLICE IS BASED ON A TRUE STORY
"WHEN SHE COME FOR YOUUUU?"

END.

We now fly to Pondgea to take an extra-special behind-the-scenes look at the creation of everyone's favorite quazy bread-loving, qwazy ducks: THE BREADWINNERS! We quizzed:

STEVE BORST

Co-creator of . . .

BREADWINNERS

+00:14:55:20
+17
An animatic from Breadwinners.

Papercutz: *What inspired you to start writing cartoons?*
Steve Borst: Honestly, it just sort of happened by going where the opportunities took me. Way back in 2003, I got a job writing promos for Nickelodeon in New York City, where I formed a lot of great relationships, which eventually led to an opportunity writing for *Mad* on the West Coast. Once I started writing cartoons, I was really inspired by the limitless possibilities of the medium. In animation, if you can imagine it, it can become a reality on screen!

Papercutz: *Did you ever watch cartoons or read comics as a kid? What were your favorites?*
Steve Borst: Oh, yeah! I loved watching cartoons. I was a child of the 80s, so I was watching stuff like *G.I. Joe, Transformers, He-Man,* and one of my personal favorites: *Dungeons & Dragons.* Unsurprising Side Note: I played a lot of *Dungeons & Dragons.*

Papercutz: *What's the process behind writing the story?*
Steve Borst: The writing process consists of three basic phases: premise, outline, and script. First, one of our writers will come up with a premise, which is just a brief description of what the story is about and how it's going to be funny. Then we have a "Story Meeting" where we flesh out the basic beats of the story with all of our writers, the director of the episode, the supervising director, and the script coordinator. The writer then goes off and writes an outline (about 3 pages). Once that's approved, the writer writes a script (about 16 pages). Eventually we get our group back together for a "Table Read" where we read the script out loud and brainstorm ways to make it even better. The Network also weighs in at all three phases with their feedback. After the script is approved, we record it with our voice-over talent. We continue to make tweaks to the script throughout the storyboarding process, and we re-record new dialogue as necessary. As you can see, it's a rather lengthy and highly collaborative party-punchin' process!

A model sheet of SwaySway

Papercutz: *What were the key personality traits that you wanted SwaySway and Buhdeuce to have?*
Steve Borst: We wanted SwaySway and Buhdeuce to both be very optimistic and enthusiastic. To differentiate the characters, we made SwaySway super confident (even if he doesn't always know what he's doing). And we made Buhdeuce super goofy. BOOTY KICK!

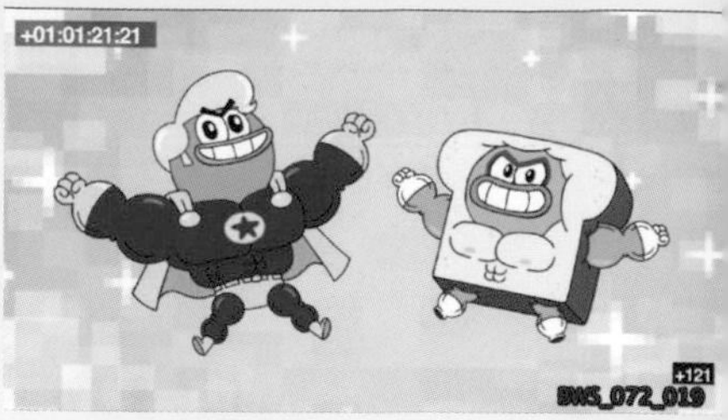
+01:01:21:21
+121
BWS_072_019

Papercutz: *Do you really like bread a lot and how did it become a big part of BREADWINNERS?*
Steve Borst: I loaf bread, but I think Gary (DiRaffaele, co-creator of BREADWINNERS) loafs it even more! It was his idea to incorporate bread into the show. We eventually decided that we wanted our bread to be special. After all, we were making a cartoon and we could do anything we wanted to! So we made up our own unique, silly types of bread like Bubblegum Rye and Huckleberry Spaghetti Bread. Later, we pushed the uniqueness of our bread even further by introducing breads that had magical effects like Love Loaf, which causes you to fall in love with the first person you see after eating it. Magical breads led us to a lot of fun story ideas!

Papercutz: *Who's your favorite character in the series and why?*
Steve Borst: SwaySway! I like his reckless enthusiasm. He's a super fun character to write.

Papercutz: *Which character do you relate to the most in the series and why?*
Steve Borst: The Bread Maker! He spends a lot of time just hanging out in his man cave coming up with crazy ideas for new types of bread. That's sort of what I like to do as a writer: just hang out in my man cave coming up with crazy ideas.

Papercutz: *Would you ever want to work with SwaySway and Buhdeuce and why or why not?*
Steve Borst: Oh, no! Definitely not! I get motion sick too easy, and those guys fly the rocket van way too quazy! I'd be yackin' up my breakfast before you could say "barrel roll."

Papercutz: *How did you meet Gary "Doodles" DiRaffaele and what made you interested in working with him in creating BREADWINNERS?*
Steve Borst: Gary and I met while we were both working at *Mad* (Warner Bros. Animation). I was a writer on the show and Gary was an animator. One day, Gary asked me if I'd like to collaborate. I showed him some scripts I had written and he showed me some shorts he had animated. We both liked each other's work, so we decided to combine our talents, kick around some ideas, and maybe make a short together. Once we started collaborating, I could tell that Gary was an amazing artist and super passionate about making cartoons.

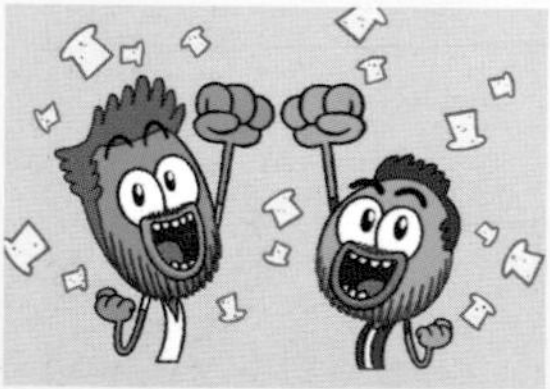

Creators Steve Borst and Gary Doodles…as ducks!

Papercutz: *How did you feel when you found out that BREADWINNERS was going to be a full-length series?*
Steve Borst: I felt warm and fuzzy for days! And it made me realize that anything is possible if you set your mind to it. Even now, I feel very grateful for being given this amazing opportunity. Thank you, Nickelodeon!

Be sure to catch our next behind-the-scenes interview with BREADWINNERS co-creator Gary "Doodles" DiRaffaele in NICKELODEON PANDEMONIUM #2!

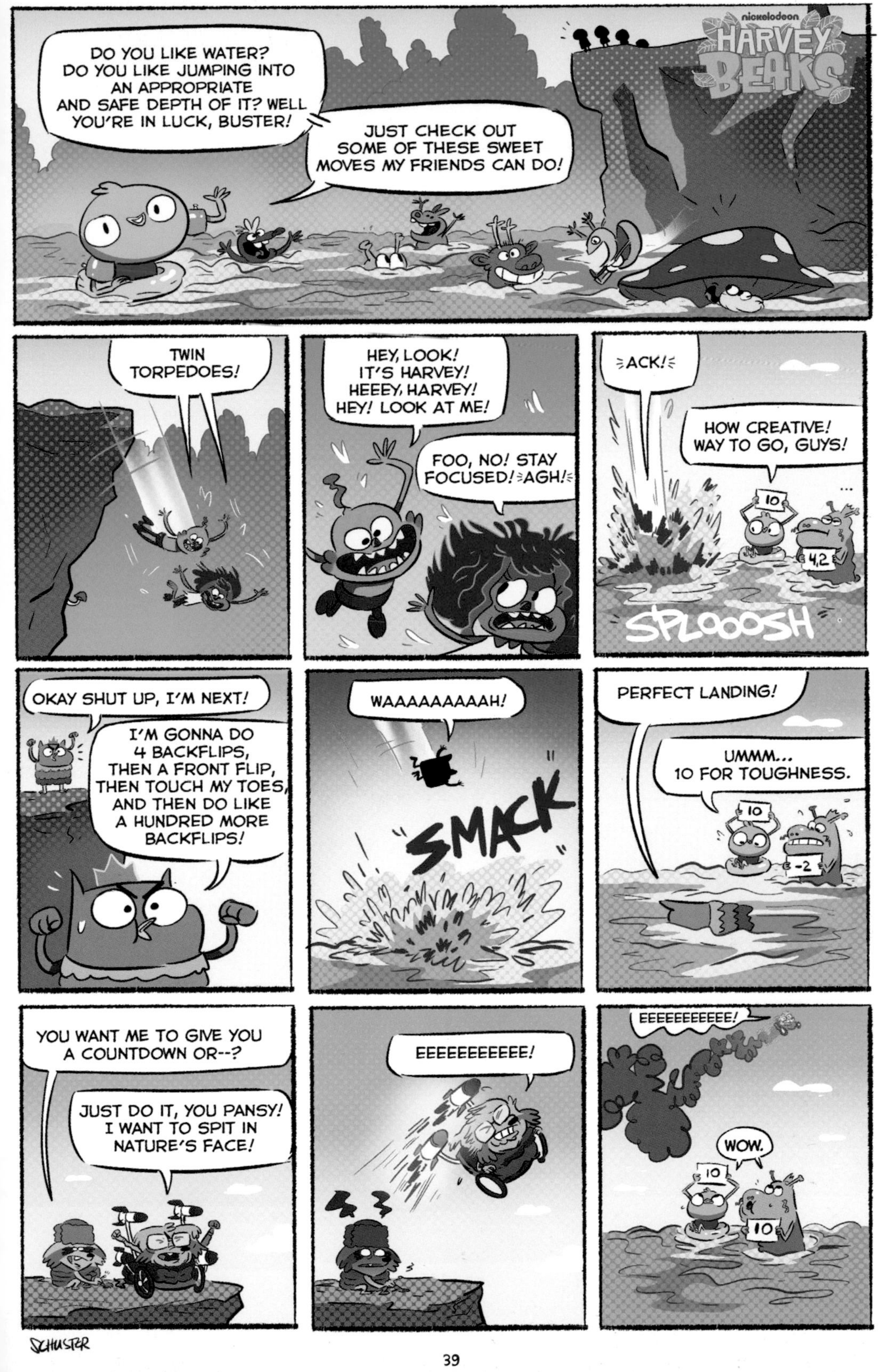
nickelodeon
HARVEY BEAKS
DO YOU LIKE WATER? DO YOU LIKE JUMPING INTO AN APPROPRIATE AND SAFE DEPTH OF IT? WELL YOU'RE IN LUCK, BUSTER!
JUST CHECK OUT SOME OF THESE SWEET MOVES MY FRIENDS CAN DO!
TWIN TORPEDOES!
HEY, LOOK! IT'S HARVEY! HEEEY, HARVEY! HEY! LOOK AT ME!
FOO, NO! STAY FOCUSED! AGH!
ACK!
HOW CREATIVE! WAY TO GO, GUYS!
10
...
4,2
SPLOOOSH
OKAY SHUT UP, I'M NEXT!
I'M GONNA DO 4 BACKFLIPS, THEN A FRONT FLIP, THEN TOUCH MY TOES, AND THEN DO LIKE A HUNDRED MORE BACKFLIPS!
WAAAAAAAAAH!
SMACK
PERFECT LANDING!
UMMM... 10 FOR TOUGHNESS.
10
-2
YOU WANT ME TO GIVE YOU A COUNTDOWN OR--?
JUST DO IT, YOU PANSY! I WANT TO SPIT IN NATURE'S FACE!
EEEEEEEEEEE!
EEEEEEEEEEE!
WOW.
10
10
SCHUSTER

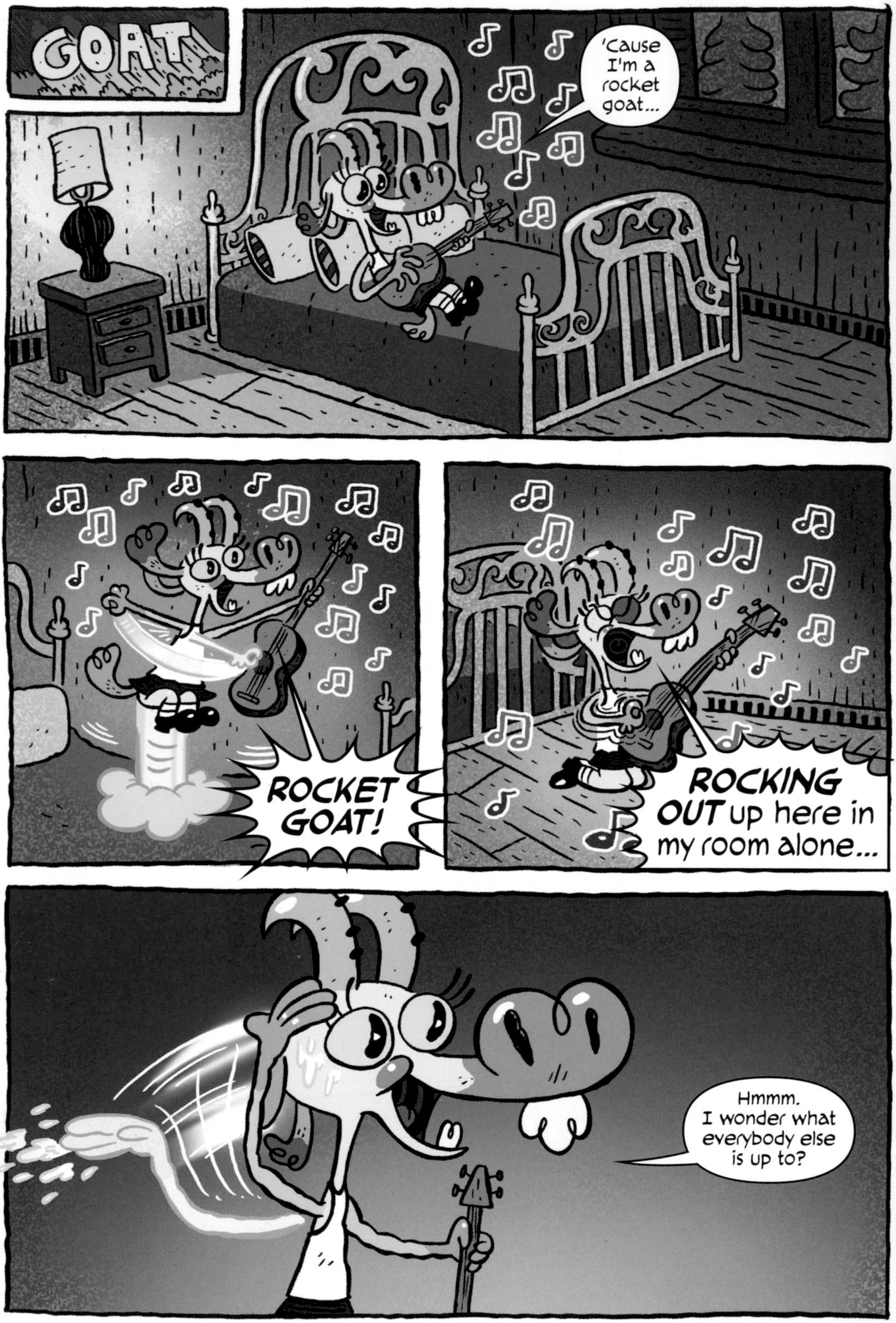
GOAT
'Cause I'm a rocket goat...
ROCKET GOAT!
ROCKING OUT up here in my room alone...
Hmmm. I wonder what everybody else is up to?

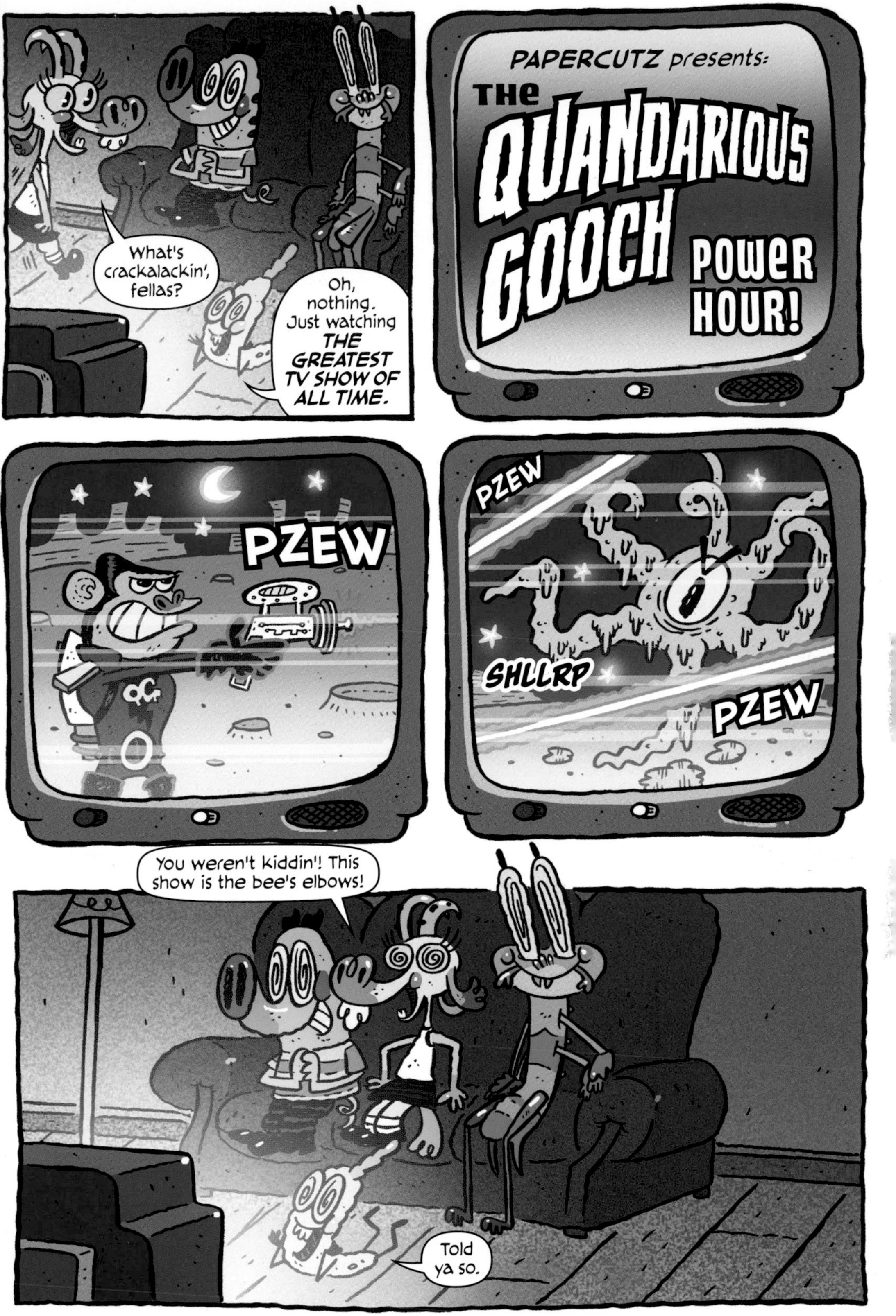
What's crackalackin', fellas?
Oh, nothing. Just watching THE GREATEST TV SHOW OF ALL TIME.
PAPERCUTZ presents:
THE QUANDARIOUS GOOCH POWER HOUR!
PZEW
PZEW
SHLLRP
PZEW
You weren't kiddin'! This show is the bee's elbows!
Told ya so.

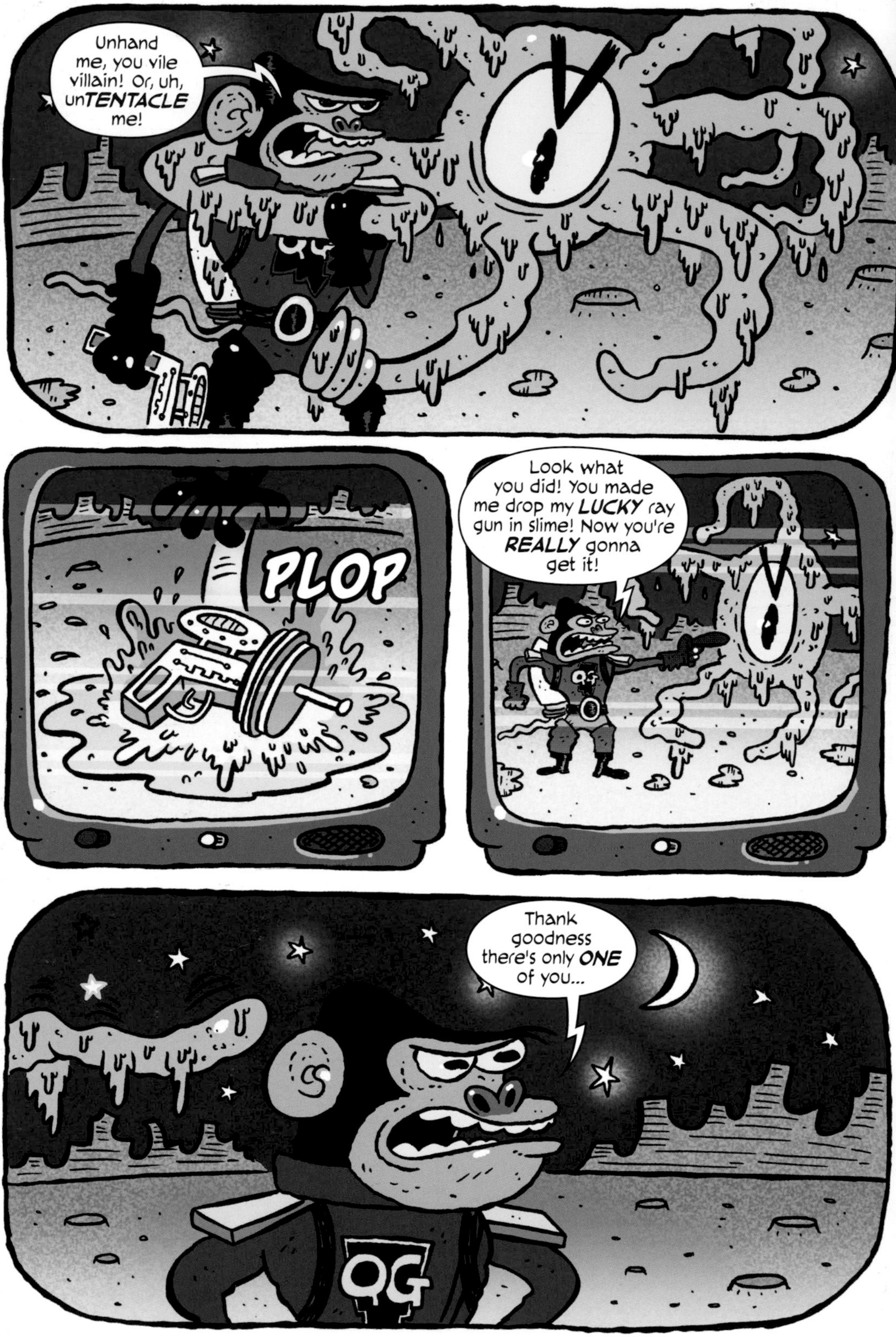
Unhand me, you vile villain! Or, uh, unTENTACLE me!
PLOP
Look what you did! You made me drop my LUCKY ray gun in slime! Now you're REALLY gonna get it!
Thank goodness there's only ONE of you...

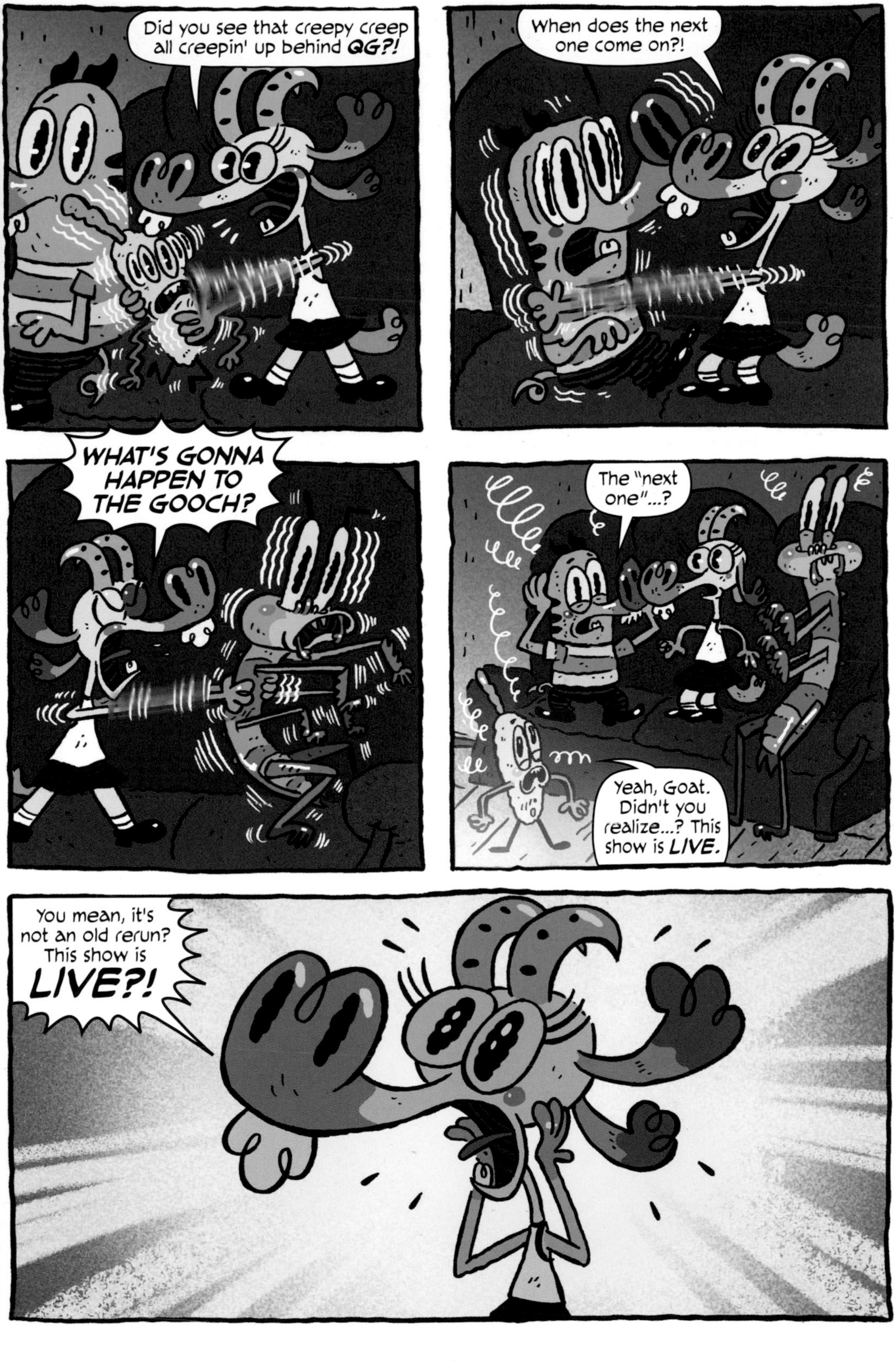
Did you see that creepy creep all creepin' up behind QG?!
When does the next one come on?!
WHAT'S GONNA HAPPEN TO THE GOOCH?
The "next one"...?
Yeah, Goat. Didn't you realize...? This show is LIVE.
You mean, it's not an old rerun? This show is LIVE?!

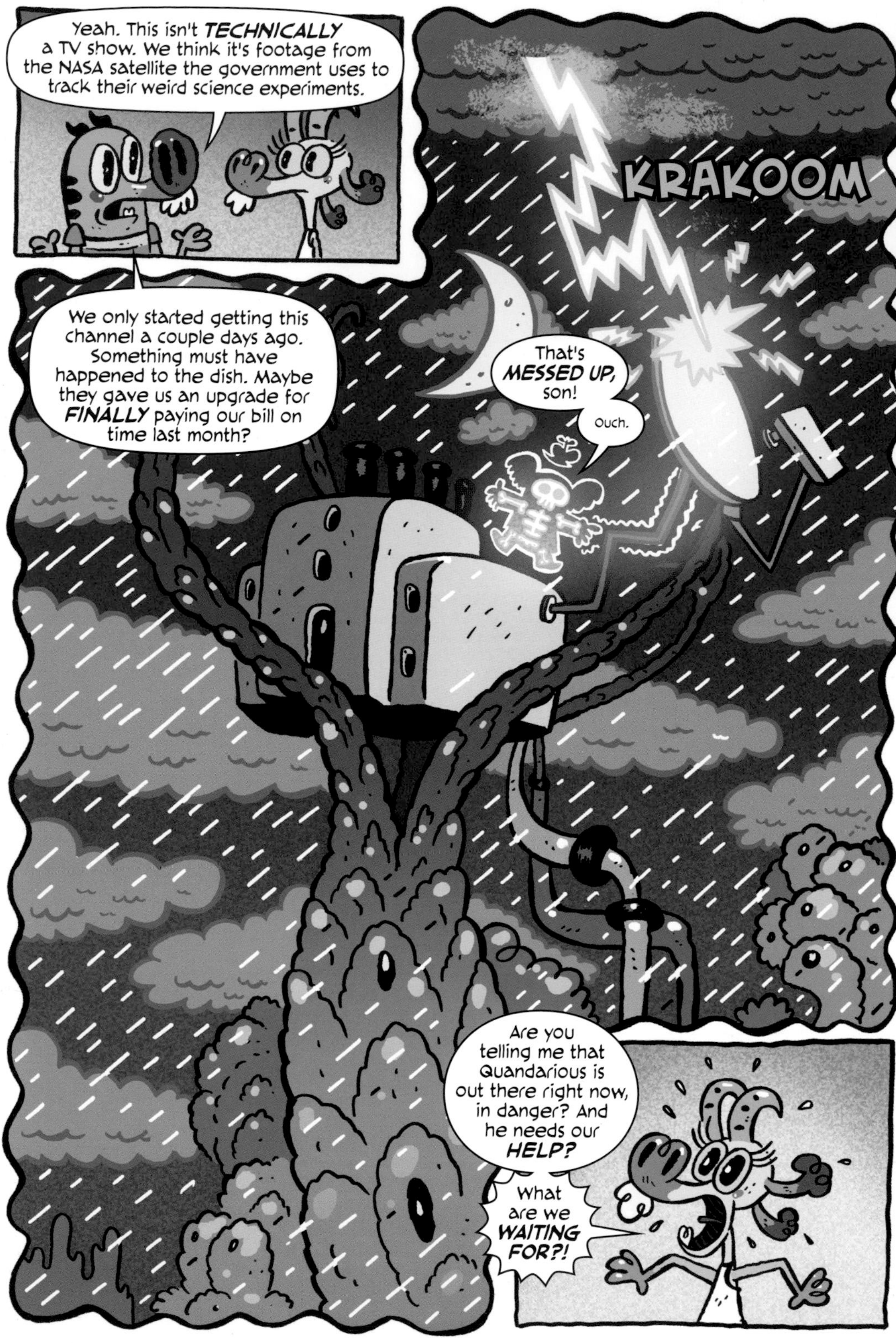
Yeah. This isn't TECHNICALLY a TV show. We think it's footage from the NASA satellite the government uses to track their weird science experiments.
KRAKOOM
We only started getting this channel a couple days ago. Something must have happened to the dish. Maybe they gave us an upgrade for FINALLY paying our bill on time last month?
That's MESSED UP, son!
Ouch.
Are you telling me that Quandarious is out there right now, in danger? And he needs our HELP?
What are we WAITING FOR?!

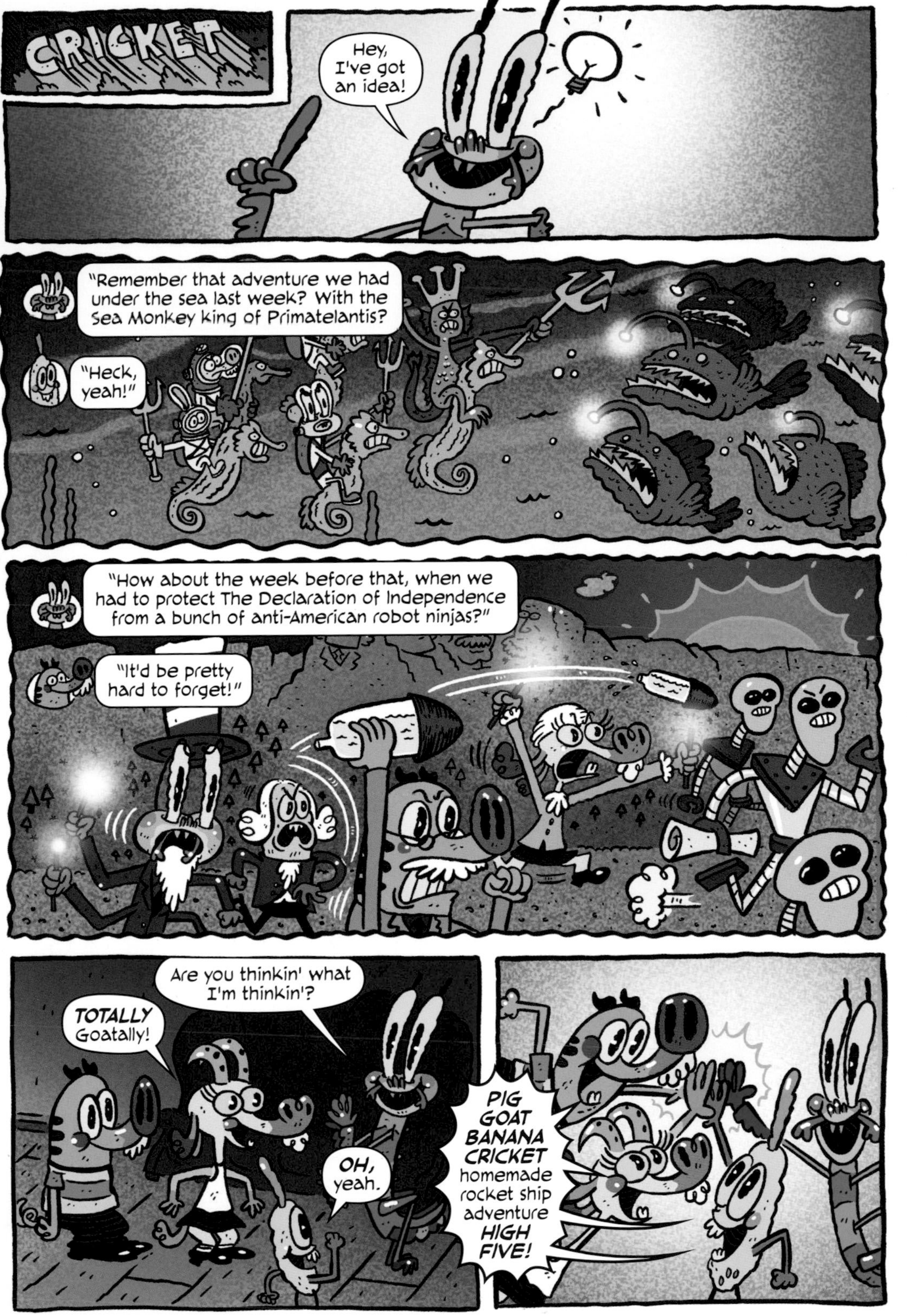
CRICKET
Hey, I've got an idea!
"Remember that adventure we had under the sea last week? With the Sea Monkey king of Primatelantis?"
"Heck, yeah!"
"How about the week before that, when we had to protect The Declaration of Independence from a bunch of anti-American robot ninjas?"
"It'd be pretty hard to forget!"
Are you thinkin' what I'm thinkin'?
TOTALLY Goatally!
OH, yeah.
PIG GOAT BANANA CRICKET homemade rocket ship adventure HIGH FIVE!

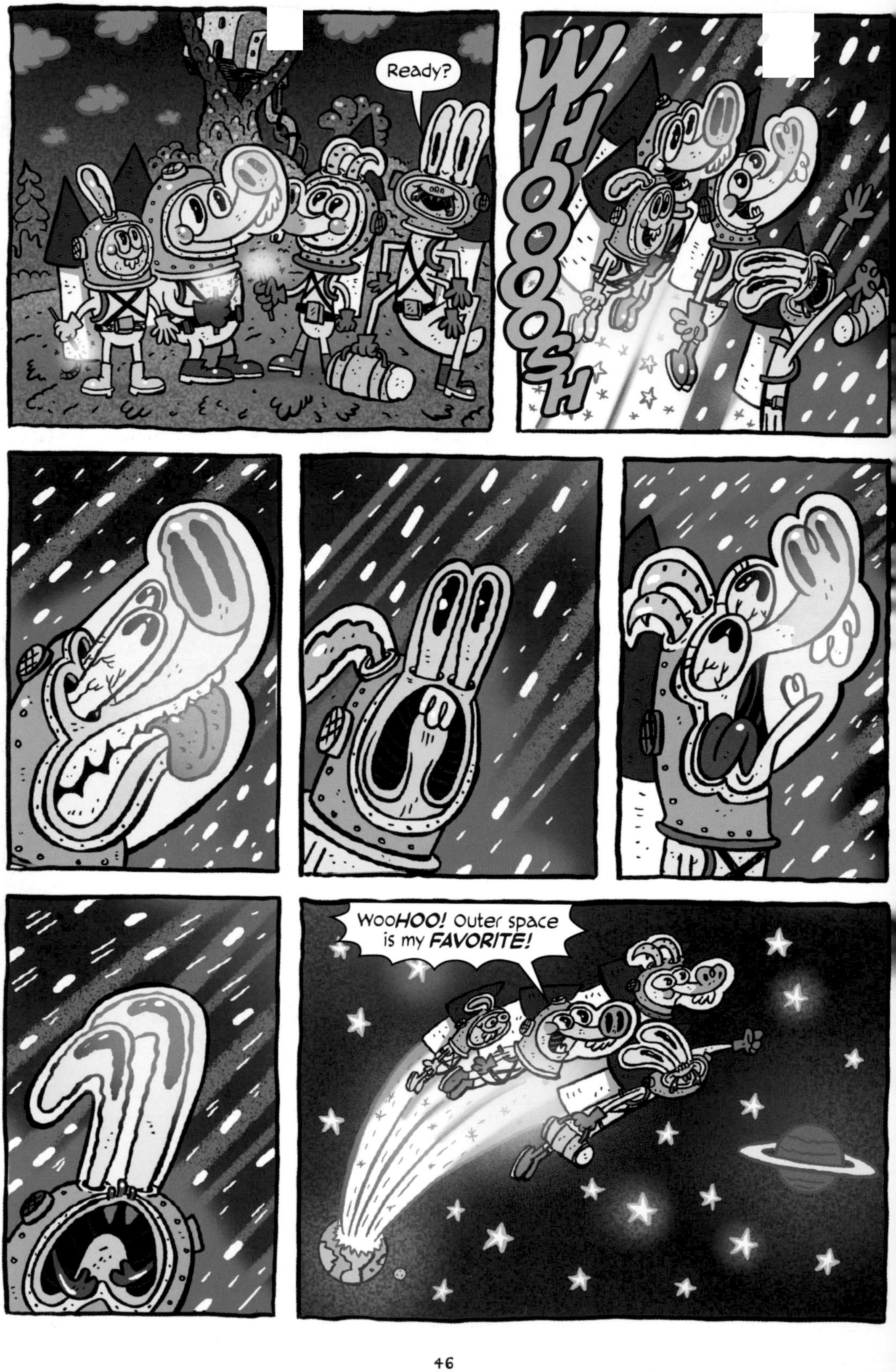
Ready?
WHOOOOOSH
WooHOO! Outer space is my FAVORITE!

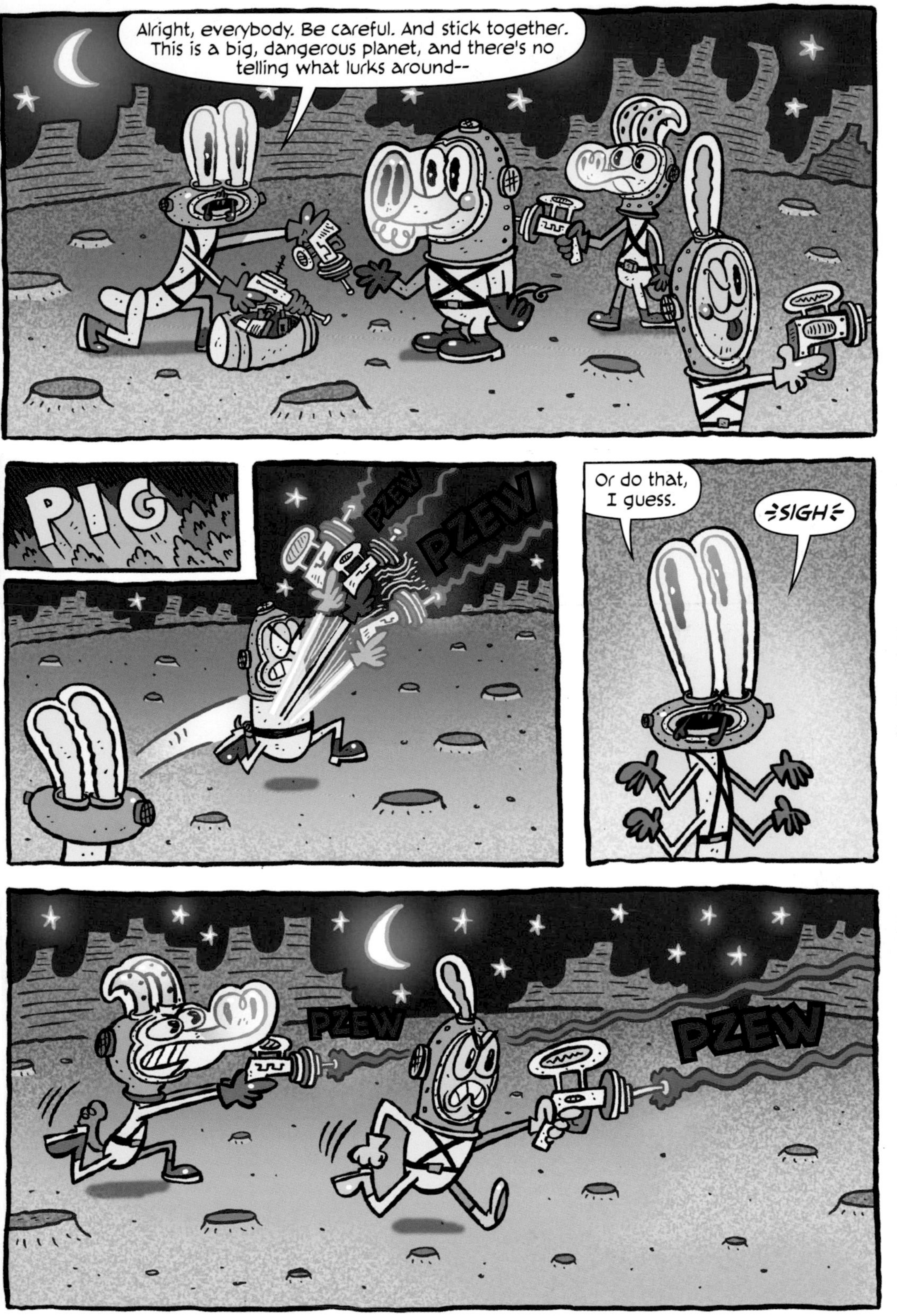

Alright, everybody. Be careful. And stick together. This is a big, dangerous planet, and there's no telling what lurks around--
PIG
PZEW
PZEW
Or do that, I guess.
SIGH
PZEW
PZEW

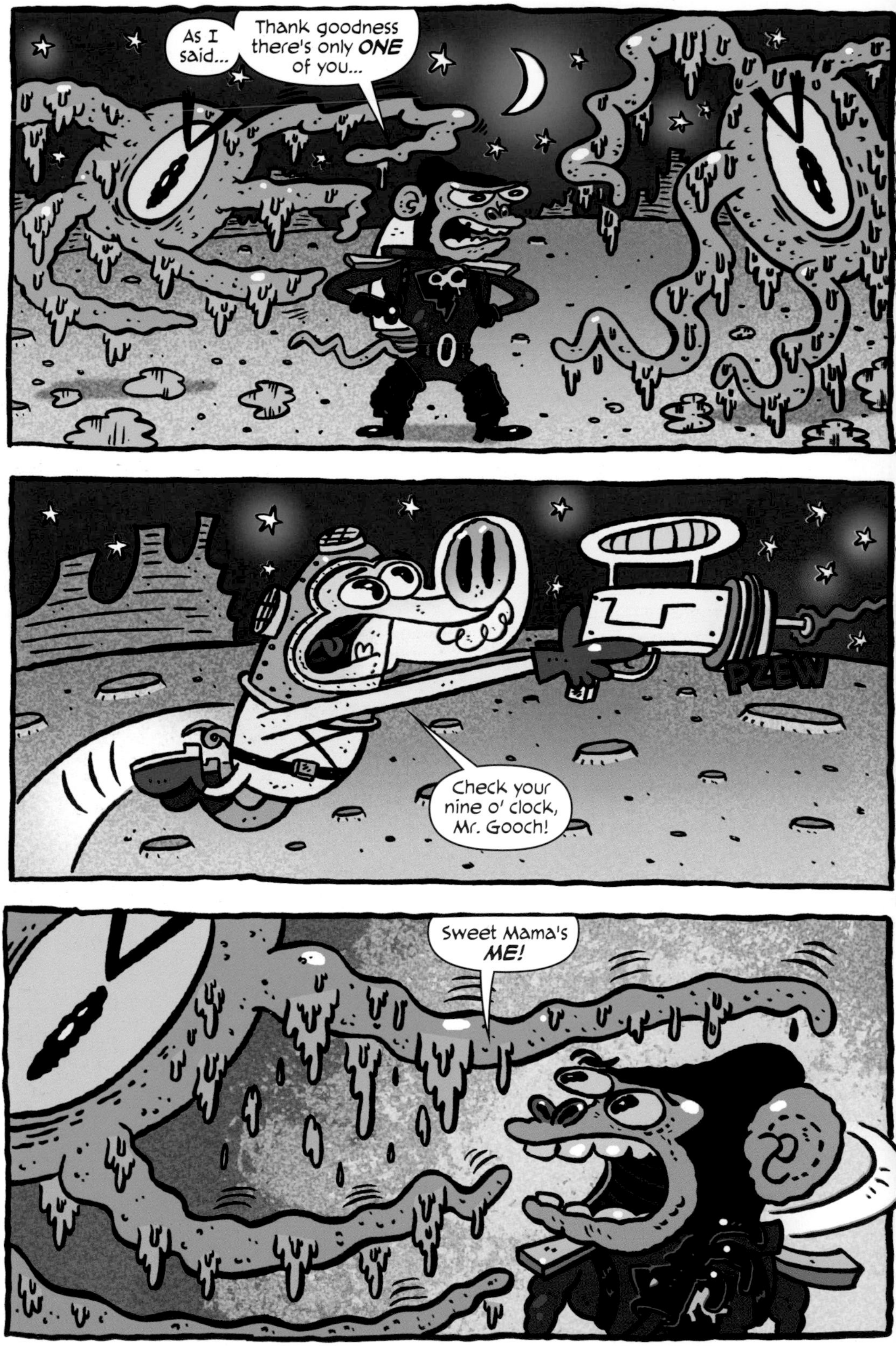
As I said...
Thank goodness there's only ONE of you...
PZEW
Check your nine o' clock, Mr. Gooch!
Sweet Mama's ME!

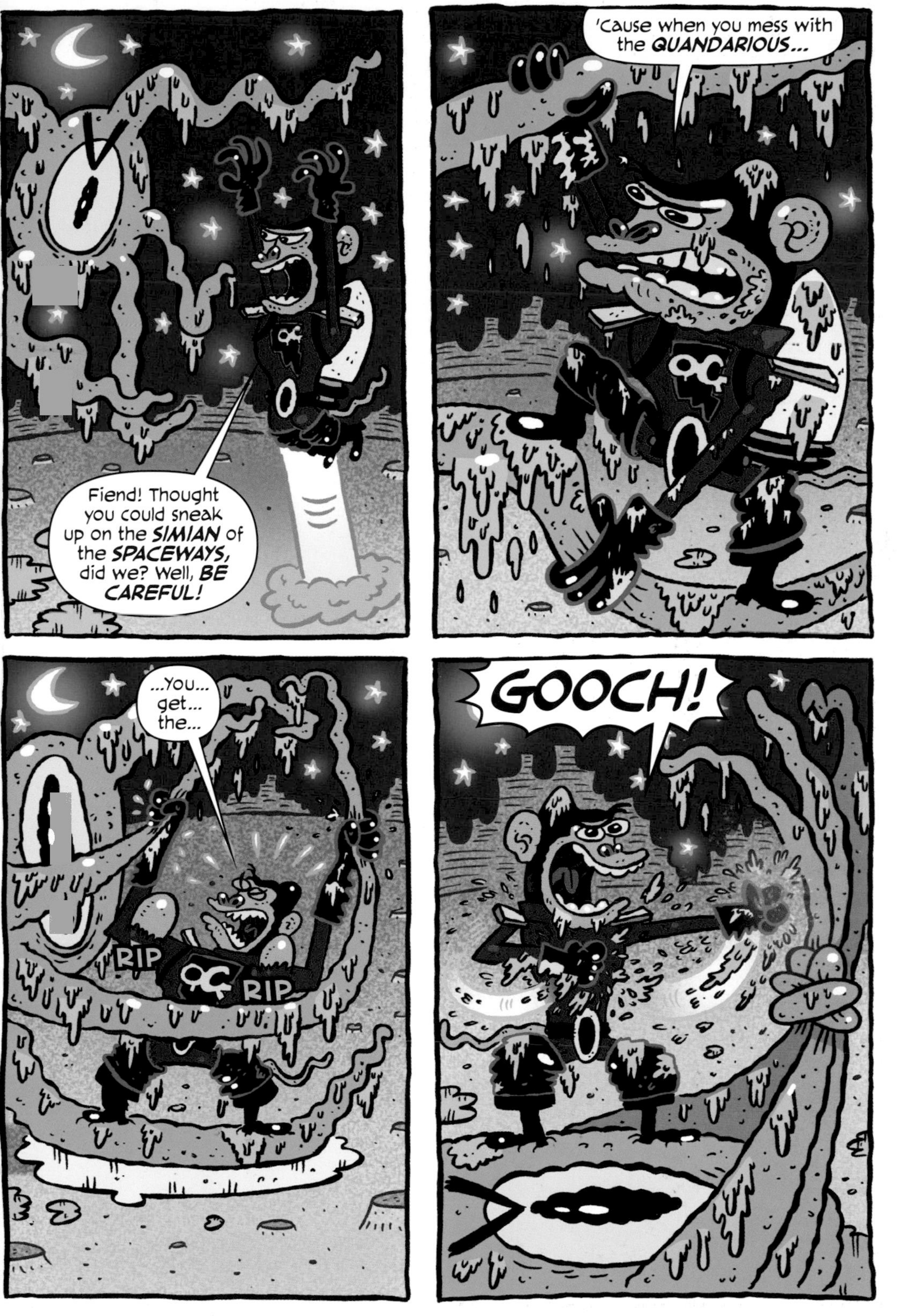
Fiend! Thought you could sneak up on the SIMIAN of the SPACEWAYS, did we? Well, BE CAREFUL!
'Cause when you mess with the QUANDARIOUS...
...You... get... the...
GOOCH!
RIP
RIP

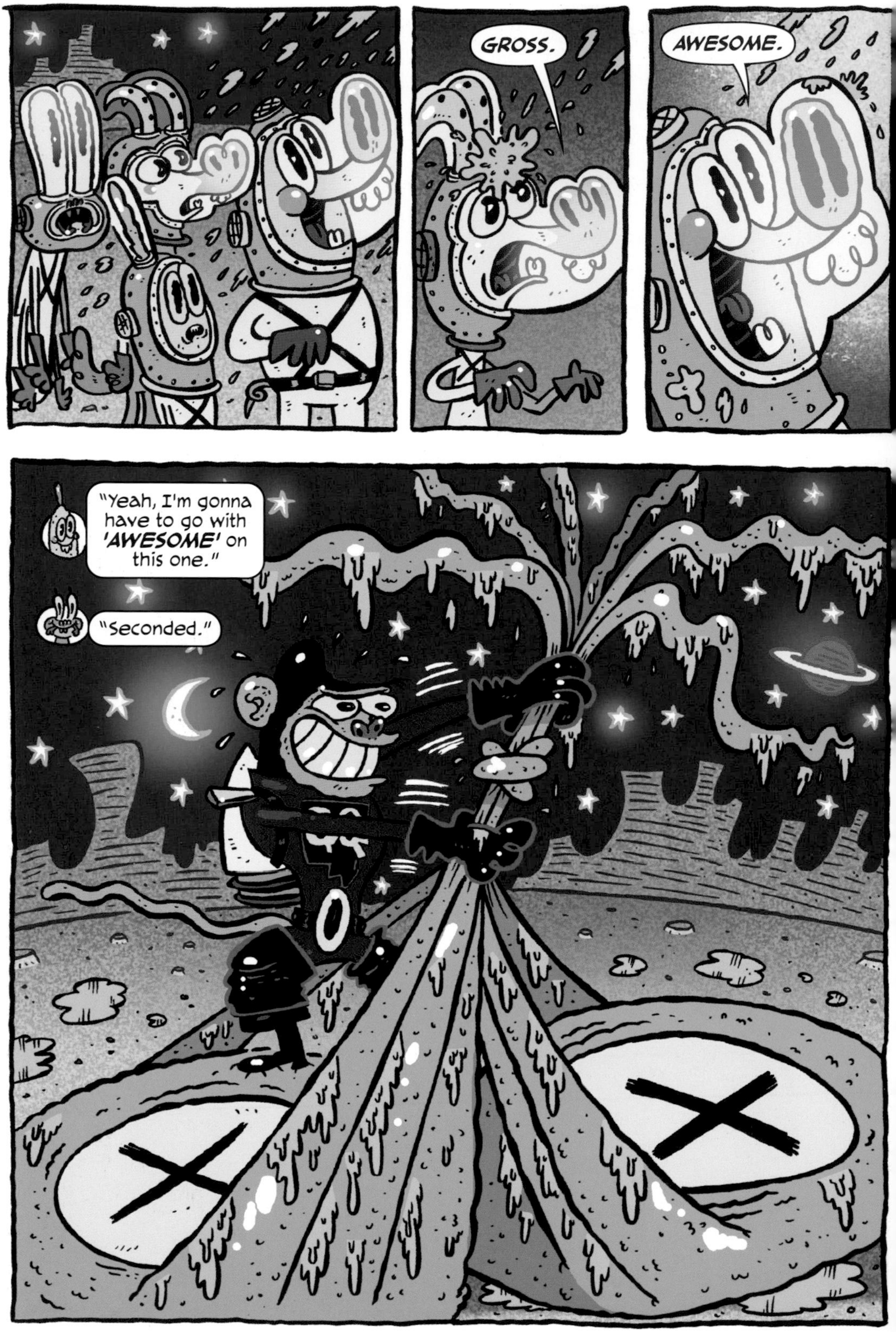
GROSS.
AWESOME.
"Yeah, I'm gonna have to go with 'AWESOME' on this one."
"Seconded."

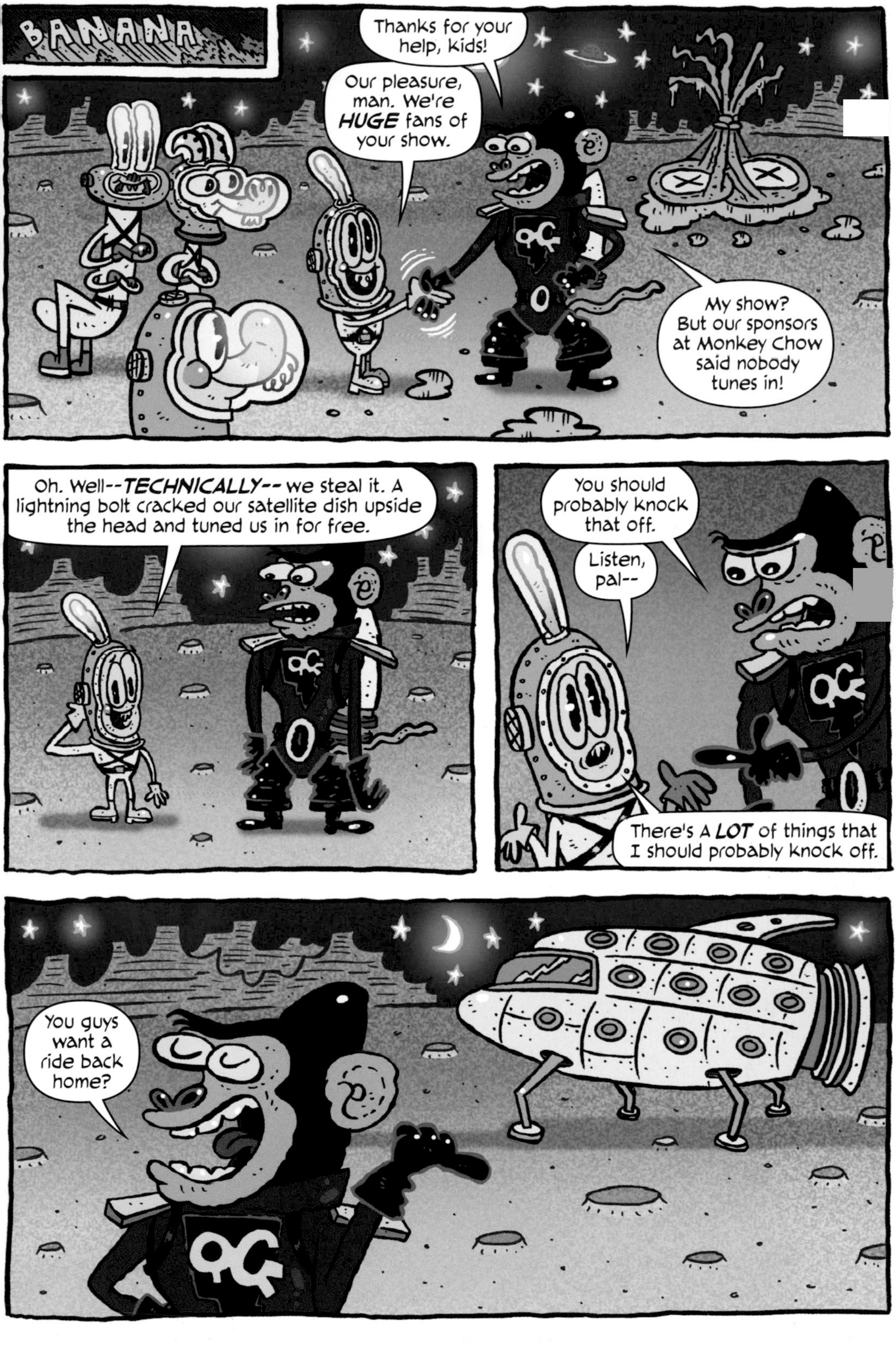
BANANA
Thanks for your help, kids!
Our pleasure, man. We're *HUGE* fans of your show.
My show? But our sponsors at Monkey Chow said nobody tunes in!
Oh. Well--*TECHNICALLY*--we steal it. A lightning bolt cracked our satellite dish upside the head and tuned us in for free.
You should probably knock that off.
Listen, pal--
There's A *LOT* of things that I should probably knock off.
You guys want a ride back home?

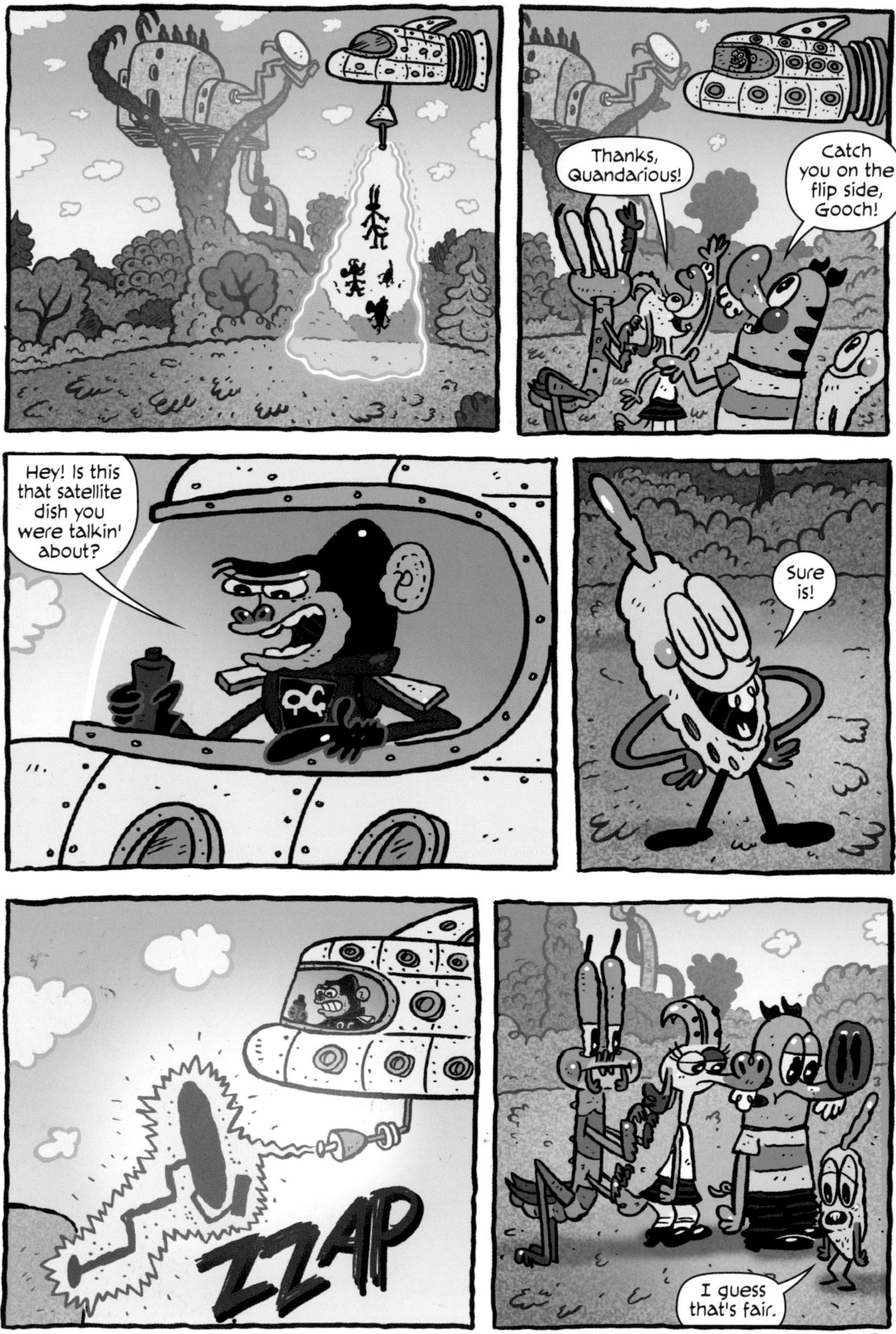
Thanks, Quandarious!
Catch you on the flip side, Gooch!
Hey! Is this that satellite dish you were talkin' about?
Sure is!
ZZAP
I guess that's fair.

END.

Want another extra-special behind-the-scenes bonus feature?
You got it! To follow up on our interview with Dave Cooper (see page 13) we talked to his PGBC partner:

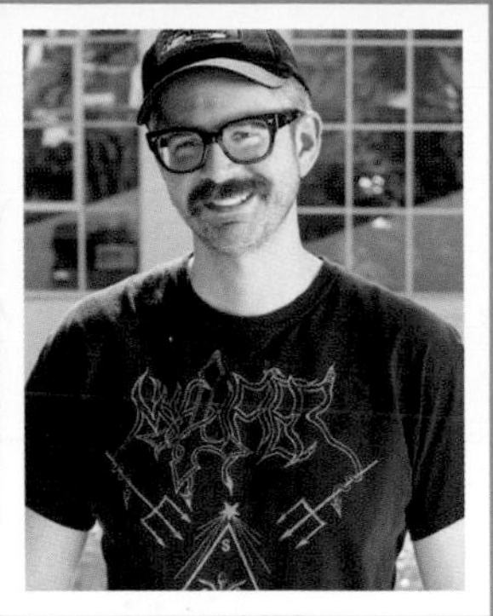

JOHNNY RYAN

Co-creator of . . .

PIG GOAT BANANA CRICKET™

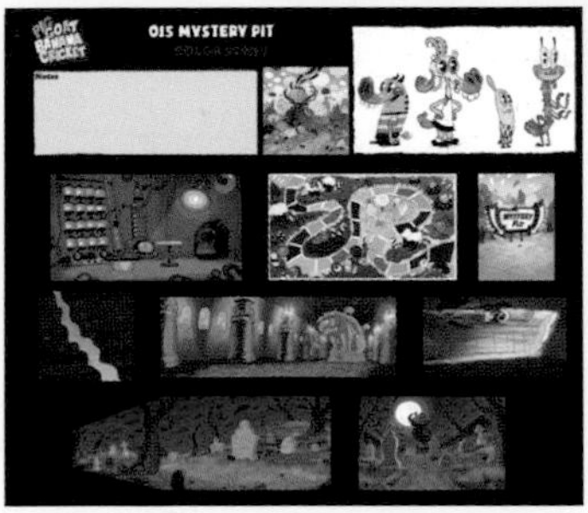
015 MYSTERY PIT

The Color Script for a PGBC episode.

Papercutz: *Did you ever watch cartoons or read comics as a kid? What were your favorites?*
Johnny Ryan: I sure did. I loved *Underdog* and *Daffy Duck* and *Deputy Dawg* cartoons. And I loved *MAD Magazine* and *SPIDER-MAN* and *Bloom County*...

Papercutz: *What inspired you to draw comics?*
Johnny Ryan: I always loved comics as a child. I knew then I wanted to grow up and be a cartoonist.

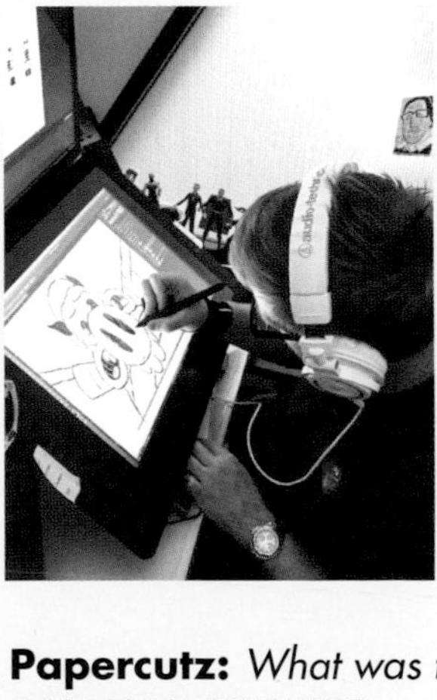

Papercutz: *How did you and PGBC co-creator Dave Cooper meet?*
Johnny Ryan: We were both invited to a comic convention in Angouleme, France. Because we were the only people there that could speak English we were forced to talk to each other.

Papercutz: *How do you and Dave come up with the jokes?*
Johnny Ryan: The jokes for the show are actually thought up by David Sacks, my co-writer, and me. And we also have a writers room filled with people who give us amazing jokes, too.

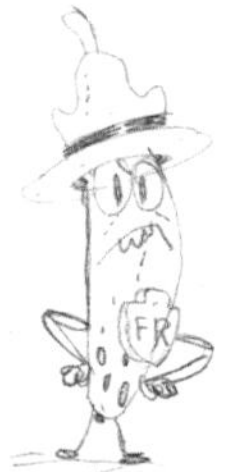

Production sketch of Banana

Papercutz: *What was the inspiration for creating PIG GOAT BANANA CRICKET?*
Johnny Ryan: It started as a comic strip Dave and I did for NICKELODEON MAGAZINE back at the turn of the century. Dave would show me a bunch of cute characters and I would give them personalities and write stories about them and then Dave would draw them up.

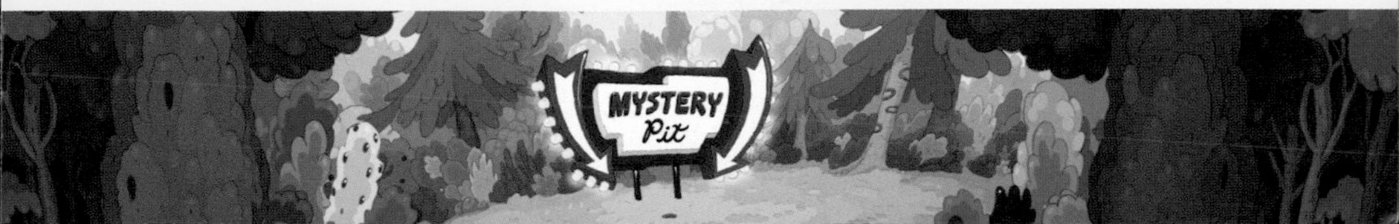
MYSTERY
Pit

Papercutz: *Have you ever lived with roommates like PGBC and if so, what was it like?*
Johnny Ryan: In college I had a couple roommates. Some were better than others.

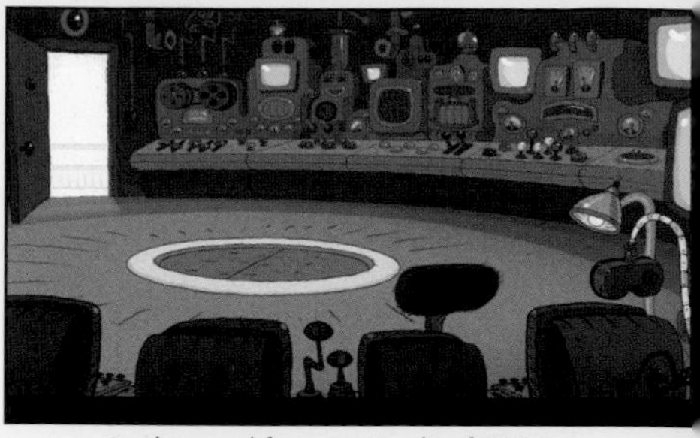

Background for an episode of PGBC.

Papercutz: *Which PGBC character do you relate to the most and why?*
Johnny Ryan: I think I relate to Angry Old Raisin the most.

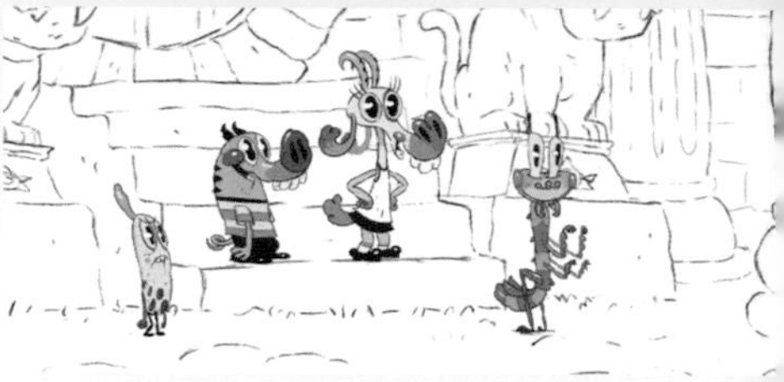

The characters are animated on a separate layer from the backgrounds.

Papercutz: *What were the ideas behind the makings of each character?*
Johnny Ryan: With Pig, I wanted to create a character that was really dumb but fun and happy at the same time. Banana was meant to be the jerk of the group. He's got this constant inner conflict going between his own self-interests and his loyalty to his friends. Goat was meant to be super sweet and positive on the surface but underneath it all she's got a hair trigger temper that gets her into a lot of trouble. And Cricket is a mixed-up genius that's kind of his own worst enemy. He's always on the verge of winning the Genius of the Year Award, but he can never quite make it happen. And his secret love of Goat will always go unrequited.

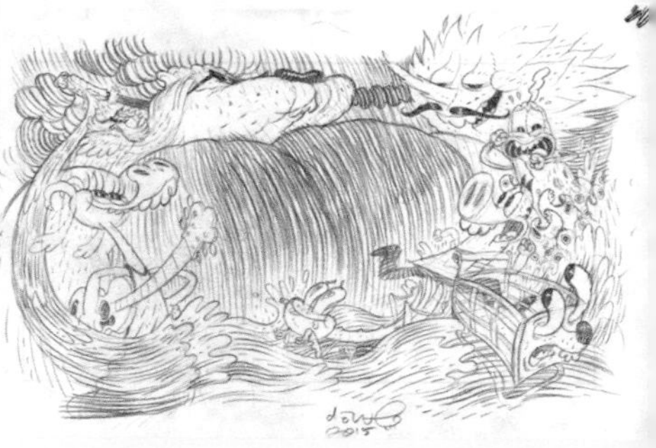

Sketches are used for episode ideas.

Papercutz: *Was there any reason why you and Dave chose to have a pig, a goat, a banana, and a cricket to live as roommates?*
Johnny Ryan: It seemed like a fun starting point for some wild adventures.

Papercutz: *Would you ever hang out with Pig, Goat, Banana, and Cricket? If so what would you do with them?*
Johnny Ryan: Sure! Probably have the world's greatest pool party!

Pig Goat Banana — Who? – Cricket was the last to be added to the team. The creators worked hard seeing who was a good fit for the crew!

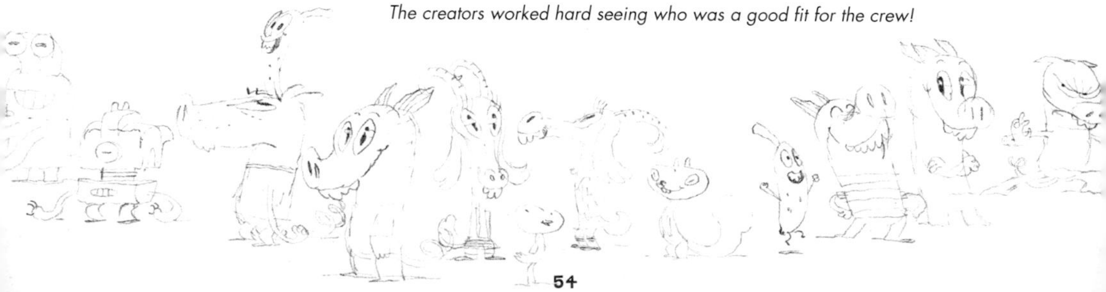

FOO FACTS: COMPUTERS!

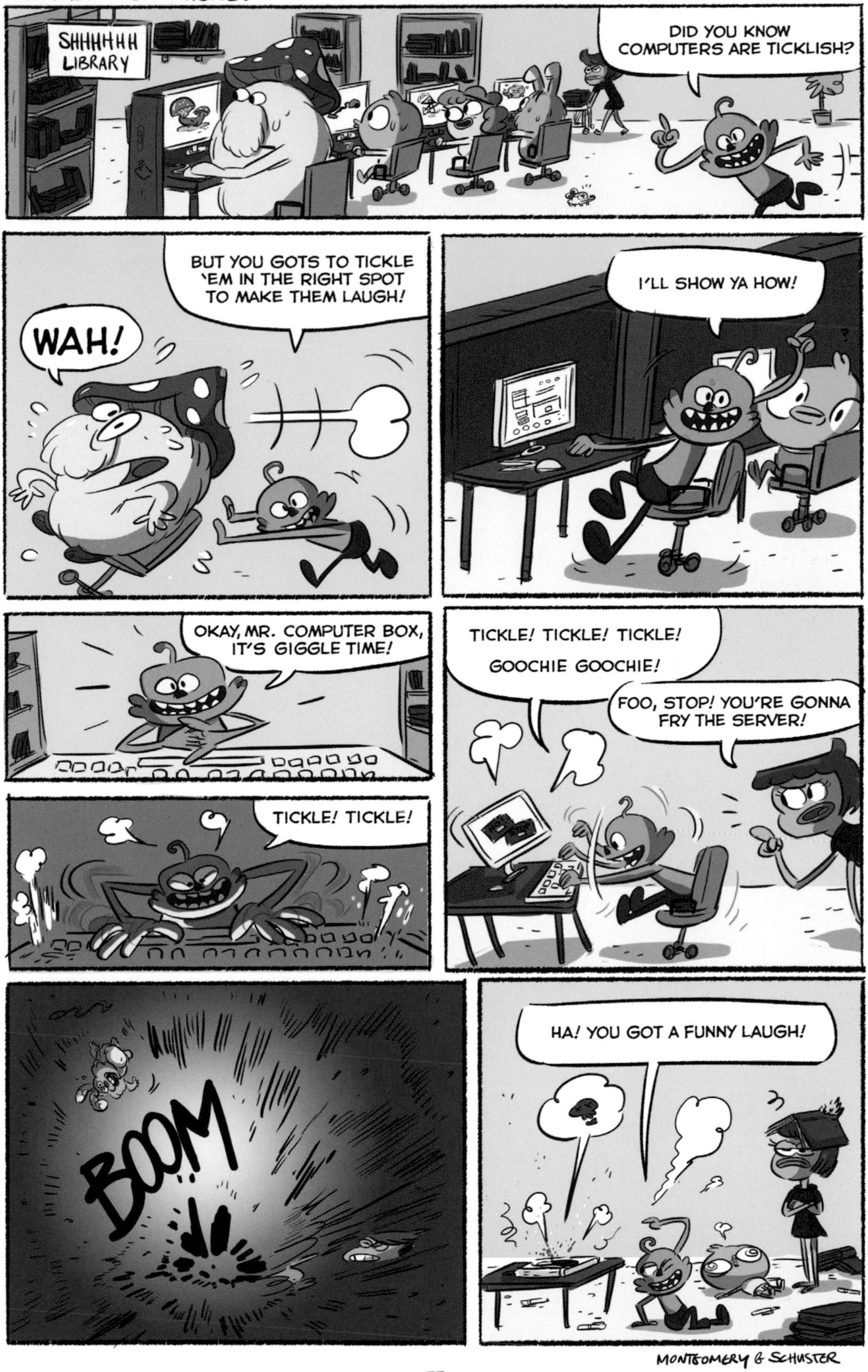
SHHHHHH LIBRARY
DID YOU KNOW COMPUTERS ARE TICKLISH?
BUT YOU GOTS TO TICKLE 'EM IN THE RIGHT SPOT TO MAKE THEM LAUGH!
WAH!
I'LL SHOW YA HOW!
OKAY, MR. COMPUTER BOX, IT'S GIGGLE TIME!
TICKLE! TICKLE!
TICKLE! TICKLE! TICKLE!
GOOCHIE GOOCHIE!
FOO, STOP! YOU'RE GONNA FRY THE SERVER!
BOOM
HA! YOU GOT A FUNNY LAUGH!

MONTGOMERY & SCHUSTER

MEET THE LOUD FAMILY!

LORI

THE OLDEST

LENI

THE BEAUTY

LUNA

THE ROCK STAR

LUAN

THE JOKESTER

LINCOLN

THE HERO

LYNN

THE SPORT

LUCY

THE EMO

LILY

THE POOP MACHINE

LOLA & LANA
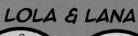

THE TWINS

LISA
THE GENIUS

THE LOUD HOUSE

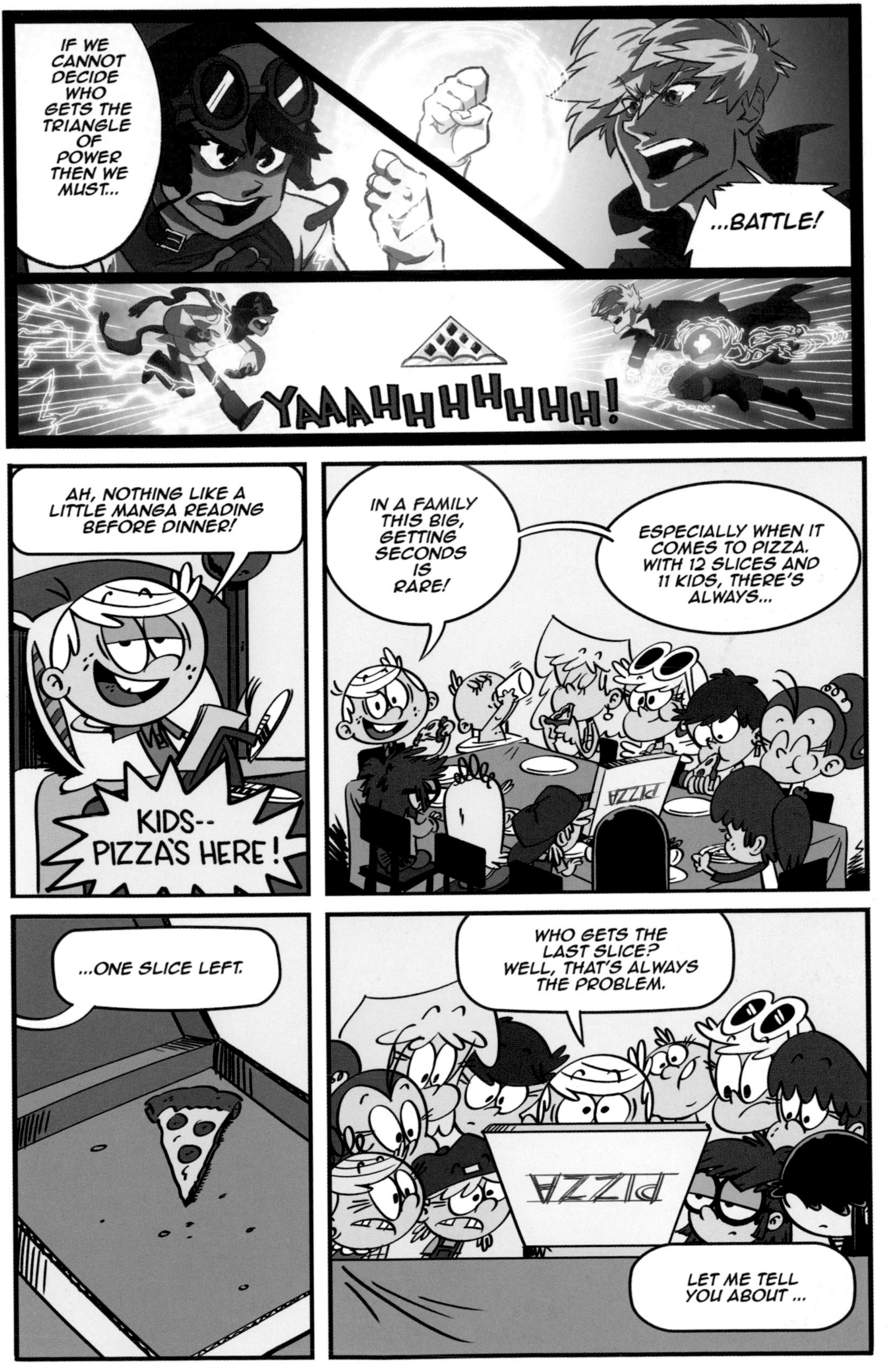

IF WE CANNOT DECIDE WHO GETS THE TRIANGLE OF POWER THEN WE MUST...
...BATTLE!
YAAAHHHHHHHH!
AH, NOTHING LIKE A LITTLE MANGA READING BEFORE DINNER!
KIDS-- PIZZA'S HERE!
IN A FAMILY THIS BIG, GETTING SECONDS IS RARE!
ESPECIALLY WHEN IT COMES TO PIZZA. WITH 12 SLICES AND 11 KIDS, THERE'S ALWAYS...
PIZZA
...ONE SLICE LEFT.
WHO GETS THE LAST SLICE? WELL, THAT'S ALWAYS THE PROBLEM.
PIZZA
LET ME TELL YOU ABOUT ...

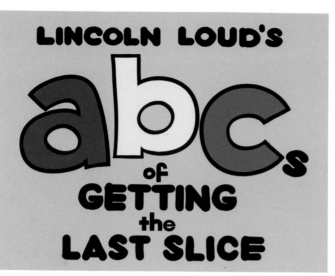

LINCOLN LOUD'S abcs of GETTING the LAST SLICE

FIRST, "a" WE ARGUE.

I'M THE OLDEST, SO I SHOULD GET IT!

NO WAY! BEAUTY BEFORE AGE!

YOU DON'T NEED IT! YOU'LL JUST EAT YOUR BOOGERS INSTEAD!

THIS IS BAD NEWS ANY WAY YOU SLICE IT! HAHAHAH! GET IT?

OH, THEN I GUESS I SHOULD GET IT!

PBTHBTH!

I KNOW! I'LL JUST CONTACT THE SPIRITS AND HAVE THEM DECIDE!

DUDE, DINNER'S KINDA CRAZY WITH A SPOOKY LITTLE GIRL LIKE YOU!

PERHAPS I CAN USE MY CALIPERS TO EQUALLY MEASURE US ALL A PIECE.

TSK, WHO NEEDS CALIPERS? ALL WE NEED TO DO IS SPLIT IT EVENLY, 40/40!

AND ARGUING NEVER WORKS.

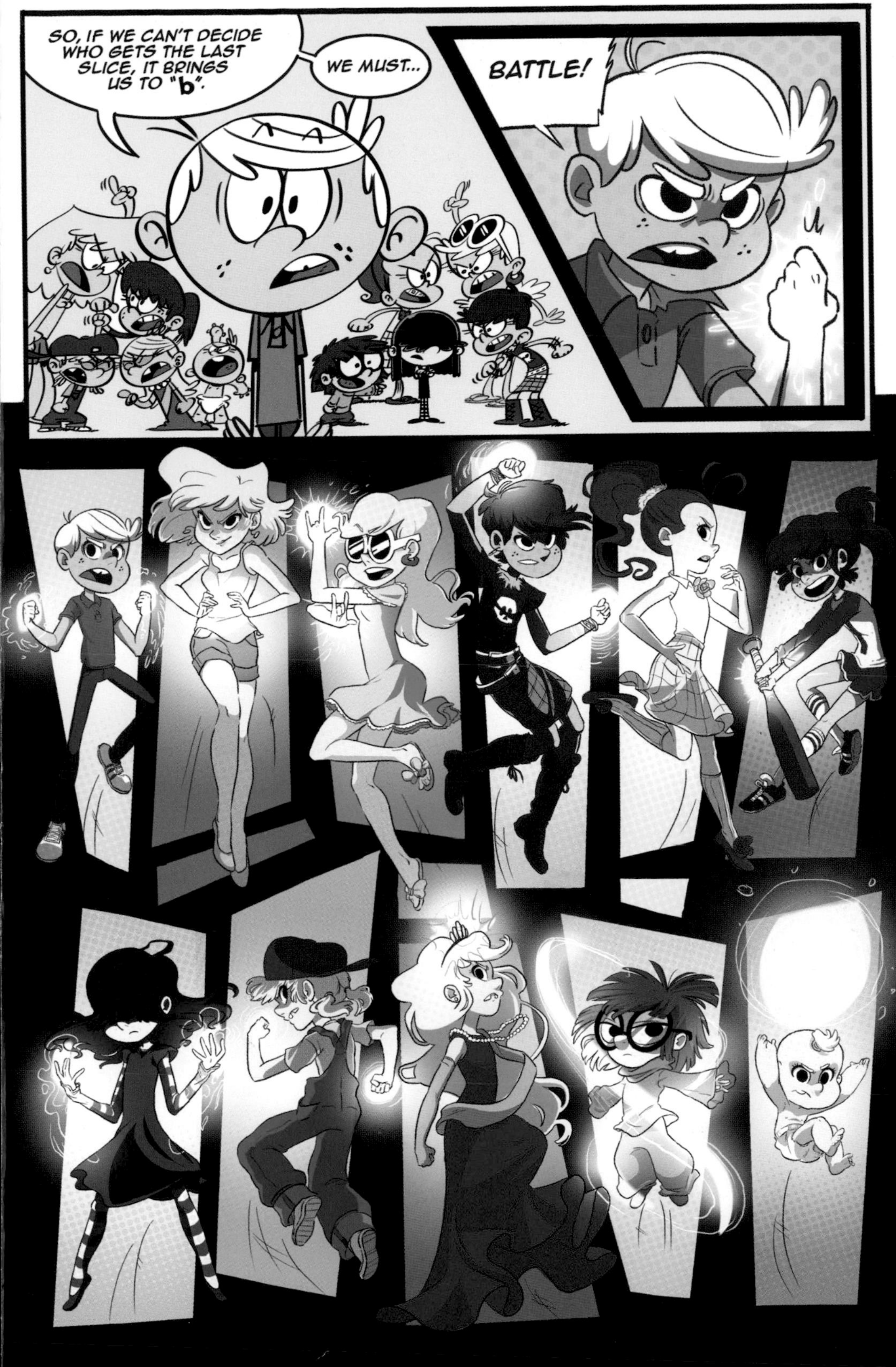
SO, IF WE CAN'T DECIDE WHO GETS THE LAST SLICE, IT BRINGS US TO "b".
WE MUST...
BATTLE!

YAAAHHHHHHHH!

YAAAHHHHHHHH!

YAAAHHHHHHHH!

YAAAHHHHHHHH!

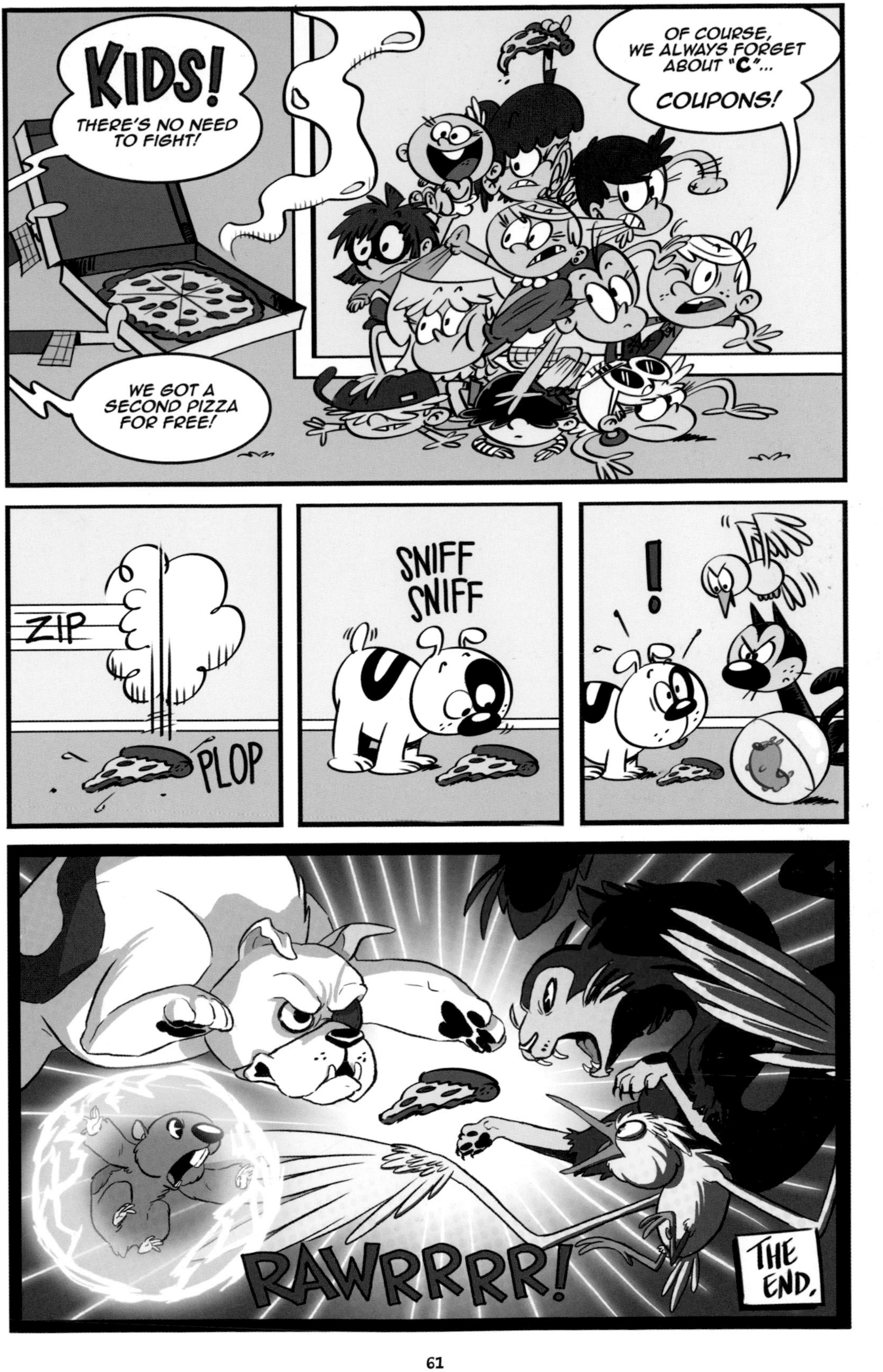
KIDS!
THERE'S NO NEED TO FIGHT!
WE GOT A SECOND PIZZA FOR FREE!
OF COURSE, WE ALWAYS FORGET ABOUT "C"...
COUPONS!
ZIP
PLOP
SNIFF SNIFF
!
RAWRRRRR!
THE END.

To close out our bonus features for this volume, we have an exclusive interview with the creator of NICKELODEON'S newest show!

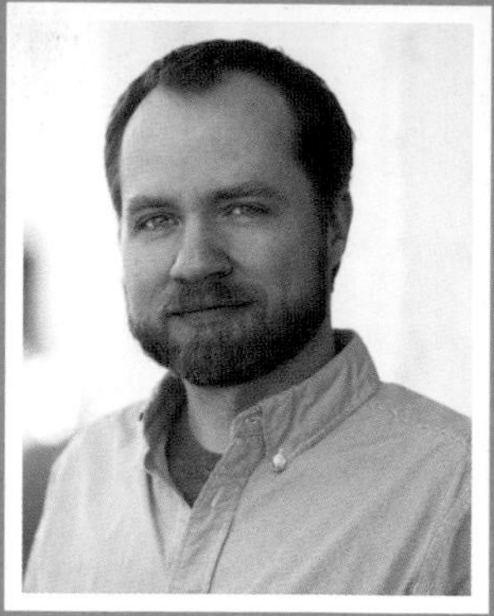

CHRIS SAVINO

Creator and Executive Producer of . . . THE LOUD HOUSE

Papercutz: *How closely are the episodes based on your real life? Did you have 10 sisters, and where did you grow up?*

Chris Savino: I am from a family with 10 kids, five boys and five girls. My sister's names all begin with "L" and each have only four letters—Lori, Lisa, Lynn, Luan, and Lana. I took those and used them for five of Lincoln's sisters. Lincoln's name comes from the street I grew up on, Lincoln Ave. in Royal Oak, Michigan – a suburb of Detroit. Little snippets of my life experiences make their way into stories, and I encourage everyone on staff to share memories as well.

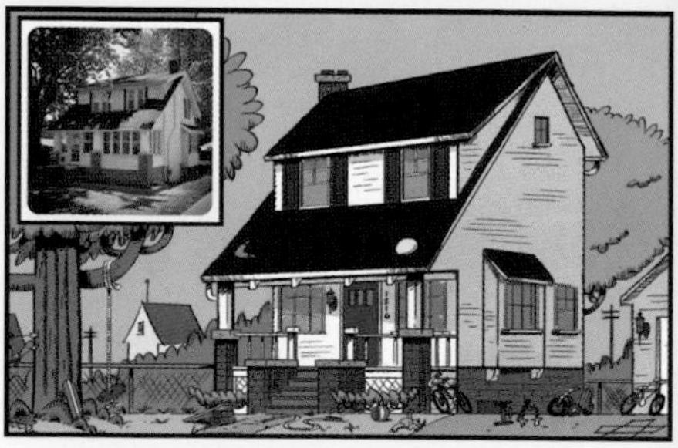

Chris Savino's childhood home inspired the Loud Family home.

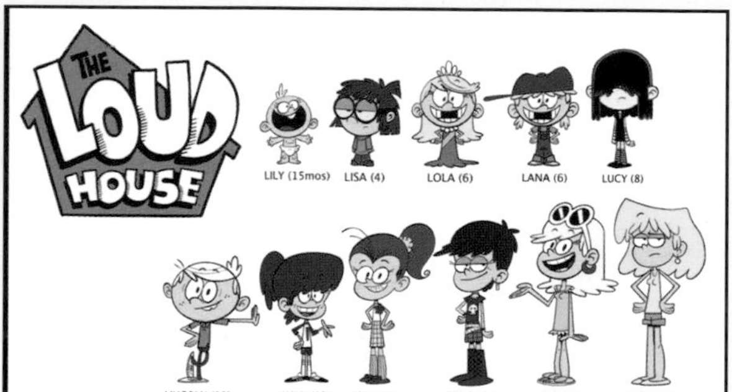
THE LOUD HOUSE
LILY (15mos)
LISA (4)
LOLA (6)
LANA (6)
LUCY (8)
LINCOLN (11)
LYNN (13)
LUAN (14)
LUNA (15)
LENI (16)
LORI (17)

Production designs for the Loud Family.

Papercutz: *Were you influenced on THE LOUD HOUSE by anything in particular?*

Chris Savino: The look of THE LOUD HOUSE is inspired by the Sunday comics I read as a kid: *Peanuts, Dennis the Menace, Garfield, Calvin and Hobbes*...There was something special about opening up the funnies and knowing that the characters you love would be there week after week inviting you into their world. That was what I wanted to achieve for THE LOUD HOUSE. A warm, familiar, and inviting environment (much like my house growing up) where you could be invited in and immediately accepted into the world where you want to hang out and get to know all of the characters.

Development sketches of Lincoln Loud.

Development sketches of Lincoln Loud.

Papercutz: *Was THE LOUD HOUSE originally envisioned as a family of rabbits? If so, why did you change this?*

Chris Savino: I thought telling the story of a boy rabbit with 25 sisters would be fun, cartoony, and chaotic. I really wanted to do funny animals, but the more I thought about it, the more I realized a human family was the right way to go. Making them human not only made the characters more relatable, but I immediately started pulling from my own life's experiences.

Papercutz: *What have you got up your sleeves for Season 2?*

Chris Savino: In Season 2, we're going to expand Lincoln's experiences and relationships outside of his home and will go more into school. The series will also take a deeper dive into the unique personalities of Lincoln's sisters.

THE LOUD HOUSE
LINCOLN LOUD

Development sketches of Lincoln Loud.

At one point Lincoln was planned to be a rabbit.

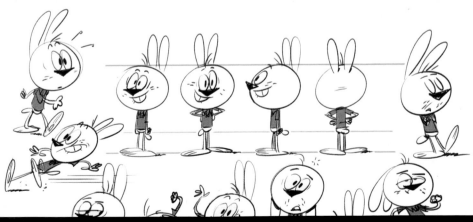

Be sure to join us in NICKELODEON PANDEMONIUM #2 for more behind-the-scenes scoops, bonus features, and, of course, comics starring your favorite cartoon characters! *Coming in 2017!*

WATCH OUT FOR PAPERCUTZ

Welcome to the premiere NICKELODEON PANDEMONIUM graphic novel from Papercutz—those couch potatoes dedicated to publishing great graphic novels for all ages. I'm Jim Salicrup, the Editor-in-Chief, future contestant on *Can You Punch That?*, and full-time Nickelodeon viewer. Yes, I'm watching Nickelodeon right now as I'm writing this! Amazing, isn't it? That may explain why, when we were deciding to come up with a very loose theme for all the comics in this collection we decided on TV. After all, who doesn't love TV? For example, when Sanjay and Craig aren't playing G&G they're usually watching TV...

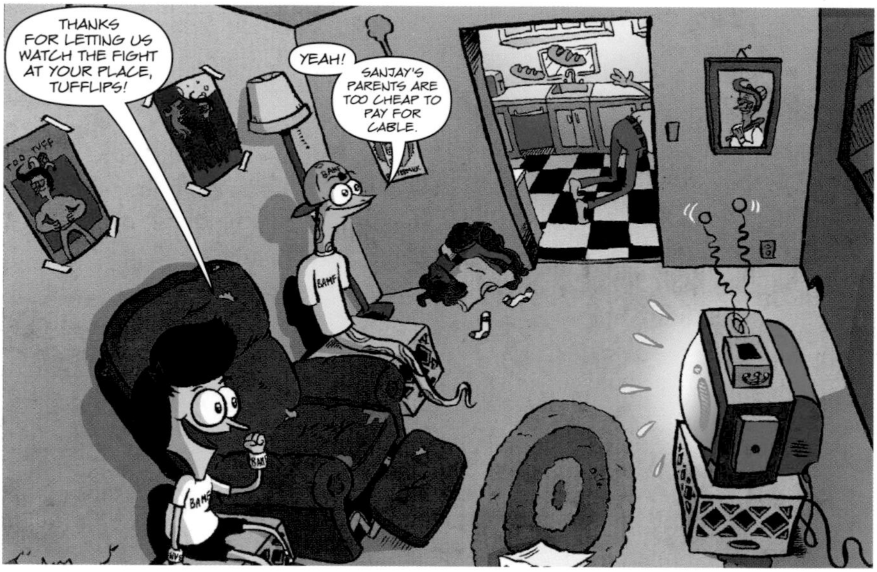
THANKS FOR LETTING US WATCH THE FIGHT AT YOUR PLACE, TUFFLIPS!
YEAH!
SANJAY'S PARENTS ARE TOO CHEAP TO PAY FOR CABLE.

Harvey Beaks, Fee, and Foo love TV so much they're able to make their own! SwaySway and Buhdeuce wind up on TV on an episode of *Tadpolice*. Pig, Goat, Banana, and Cricket certainly enjoy the *Adventures of Quandarious Gooch.* And Lincoln Loud clearly enjoys anime.

Waitaminnit! Lincoln Loud of *The Loud House*? The new big hit Nickelodeon show?! That Lincoln Loud? That's correct! We thought we'd slip him in with our usual line-up of Nickelodeon super-stars as our way of subtly announcing that we'll soon be publishing THE LOUD HOUSE as an all-new series of graphic novels. There—now aren't you happy you read this silly page all the way to the end?

Thanks, Jim

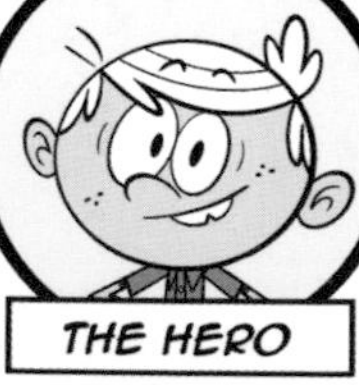
THE HERO

STAY IN TOUCH!

EMAIL:	salicrup@papercutz.com
WEB:	papercutz.com
TWITTER:	@papercutzgn
FACEBOOK:	PAPERCUTZGRAPHICNOVELS
FANMAIL:	Papercutz, 160 Broadway, Suite 700, East Wing, New York, NY 10038